Gabriel

Gabriel

by Jean Slaughter Doty

Illustrated by Ted Lewin

MACMILLAN PUBLISHING CO., INC.
New York
COLLIER MACMILLAN PUBLISHERS
London

MACMILLAN PUBLISHING CO., INC.
866 Third Avenue, New York, N.Y. 10022
Collier-Macmillan Canada Ltd.

Library of Congress catalog card number: 73–6045

Printed in the United States of America

1   2   3   4   5   6   7   8   9   10

Library of Congress Cataloging in Publication Data
Doty, Jean Slaughter, date
Gabriel.

[1.   Dogs—Fiction]   I.   Lewin, Ted, illus.   II.   Title.
PZ7.D7378Gab   [Fic]   73–6045   ISBN 978-1-4424-8609-6

TO
Wynfomeer's Cover Story
AND TO HER SON,
Champion
Rockrimmon Lord Jim
—WHO STARTED IT ALL FOR ME.

3 *days*

1 "I hate this place!" Linda stood at the window of the small living room and stared angrily at the woods and the rutted lane leading across the fields to the road. "It's dreary and ugly, and there's nothing to do."

There was a silence in the room so complete that when the pencil point broke, it sounded like an explosion.

Linda's mother reached for the pencil sharpener on her desk. A pile of papers, brushed by her arm, slid untidily to the floor. With a muffled exclamation, Mrs. Fairfax jumped to her feet.

"Out!" she said. "I simply cannot work with you

1

pacing up and down in here like a bad-tempered cat. I know you don't like it here. You've made that perfectly clear. Many times. Ever since we came here—and that was two months ago! But we are not going back to New York until my book is finished. You know very well we simply don't have enough money. . . ." Mrs. Fairfax ran her fingers tiredly through her hair. "Linda, try, just *try*, to be patient and understand."

Linda whirled from the room, snatched her jacket from the hook in the hall, and fled, slamming the front door behind her.

It had been raining all day, but now the purple clouds were blowing across the sky above the woods. The paths and ditches were brimming and overflowing into the stream which ran beside the rutted road.

Linda yanked her jacket closer around her neck and buttoned the top button with cold, impatient fingers. She hated the clumsy leather jacket just as she hated everything to do with her new life in the country. She hated the dark, bare woods and soggy fields and the shabby red house her mother had rented for a year—a whole year—miles and miles away from anything that really mattered.

Linda stamped angrily through the shining puddles left by the rain and then shuddered as the cold water stung her bare legs. Her thin blue leather shoes were streaked with mud. She glared down at them with bitter satisfaction. They were ruined now, of course, but what difference did it make? Nobody out here would see them. There was nothing here but sheep and cows and a few crummy kids at the local school whose biggest interest seemed to be rushing home to feed a calf or a horse or a bunch of pigs. . . .

A *year*. While her mother worried about money and tried to finish that darned book, giving up a perfectly good job in New York and their apartment and moving all the way out here just because the rent was cheap and everything was quiet. . . .

Linda's gray eyes filled with tears. She missed her father, who had died in a car accident almost two years ago. She missed New York, and all her old friends. . . .

She stopped. The wind had dropped, the last heavy clouds had boiled away toward the horizon, and pale streaks of late sunlight made patterns of light in the woods beside the road.

Puzzled, Linda raised her head and listened with fierce concentration. She was sure she had heard something—a thin little squeaking sound—but it had stopped.

It was getting colder by the minute. Linda hunched her shoulders inside the furry lining of her jacket and wished, briefly, that she'd worn slacks.

There. She had heard it again. She held her breath. It might only have been tree branches rubbing against each other, squeaking in the wind. It was hard to tell, especially above the rushing sound of the swollen stream.

She pushed a strand of dark hair away from her face and narrowed her eyes against the glare of the setting sun. She couldn't hear anything now. She started to turn back toward the house but then, shrugging her shoulders at her own stubbornness, she stopped to listen once more.

The thin little sound came again, unlike any she'd ever heard before. Curious and determined, she plunged into the rain-sodden woods. Vines snarled around her bare legs. Tree branches whipped across her face and she lost one shoe in the mud. She stopped, hopping on one foot, and slid the clammy shoe back on.

She pushed through a thick patch of bushes and half fell into a narrow clearing. The tree branches were heavy overhead and the light was growing dim. She could barely see the outline of a fallen tree and a blurred gray shape curled up beside it.

The gray shape moved a little and lifted its head. Linda walked over to it slowly with her heart racing. Perhaps it was a wolf—it looked like one—or maybe a

4

gray fox, though it looked too big for a fox. Linda stopped nervously. Maybe whatever it was felt trapped by her presence, and would suddenly jump to its feet and attack her.

The animal put its head down again. Its heavy gray coat was matted and soaking wet. In spite of the cold, it was panting heavily. As Linda hesitated, ready to run, it turned its head and whimpered, and wagged its shaggy tail. Linda smiled with relief and with amusement at her own foolishness. It was only a dog, of course!

The odd, shrill little squeaking sound came again, sharp and demanding. The dog tried to get up, but it was too weak. It sank back into its bed of soggy leaves.

With a soft murmur of pity, Linda hurried to the dog and sank to her knees beside it. There was another sharp squeak and the dog, with enormous effort, tried to curl up. Linda saw, with a gasp of surprise, a tiny black puppy snuggled close and dry between the dog's front legs, under its shaggy ruff.

Linda paused for a moment, still half-afraid of the dog, but it had started to shiver now and seemed almost past caring. Linda stretched out her hands and lifted the warm little black creature into her lap.

Linda had never seen a newborn puppy before. She stared at it in wonder, then swiftly cupped it in her

hands to keep it warm, and stood up. She glanced up through the branches above her. It would be dark soon and there was no time to go and get help. She was afraid she couldn't find this hidden clearing again; it would have been hard enough, even in daylight, if it hadn't been for the tiny cries of the puppy to lead her to it.

She placed the puppy gently into the deep, wool-lined pocket of her coat, then spoke softly to its mother. The dog managed to twitch her tail in response. Linda reached down and lifted the soaked, shaking dog in her arms.

She started to go, then turned and hurried back to the fallen log. She knew dogs often had more than one puppy; perhaps there were more lying there in the cold, wet leaves. But a quick, thorough search produced no more puppies. Ducking her head against the wind, which was rising again, Linda struggled back through the woods, cradling the limp gray dog in her arms.

The dog was so thin she didn't weigh very much, but, even so, Linda was glad to get out of the heavy underbrush onto the road. She walked as quickly as she could. She was gasping for breath and her arms were trembling as she stumbled up the front steps of the house.

7

"Mother!" she shouted. "Let me in!"

The door swung open and a welcome flood of light and warmth spilled out into the growing darkness. "What on earth. . . ." Mrs. Fairfax stepped back as Linda blinked up at her and tried to shake her wind-blown hair out of her eyes. "I found a dog," she said breathlessly. "In the woods . . ."

Mrs. Fairfax hurried Linda into the house and closed the door. "Take the poor thing into the kitchen," she said. "It's warmer in there. I'll get some towels."

In a few moments the shivering, panting dog was lying on one heavy towel while Mrs. Fairfax rubbed her briskly with another. "Take off your coat, Linda, and put it on the chair," Mrs. Fairfax said over her shoulder.

"Just a second," said Linda. "Wait 'til you see what else I've got." She took the tiny black puppy out of her pocket and knelt beside her mother. "Look," she said. "Just look what else I found."

Mrs. Fairfax stopped rubbing the dog for a stunned moment. "A puppy," she said softly. "Why, it can't be more than a few hours old. Were there any more?"

Linda put the puppy down on a corner of the towel and struggled out of her damp coat. "No. I thought of

8

that, and I looked, but I couldn't find any more." The puppy squirmed and squeaked restlessly.

"Poor little mite," Linda's mother said with concern. "It must be terribly hungry. Give the puppy to its mother, Linda. She's awfully thin and tired . . . let's hope she has enough milk for him."

The puppy tried frantically to nurse but it was soon obvious that the exhausted mother had almost no milk at all.

"What are we going to do?" Linda said anxiously.

"We're going to have to try to feed him ourselves," said Mrs. Fairfax. "There's some evaporated milk on the shelf. We'll mix some with a little warm water and give it to him with a medicine dropper—there's one in the bathroom cabinet. I thought I had everything we needed for a long winter, but I didn't include a baby bottle in my list!"

Linda hurried to get the dropper and then mixed the milk in a bowl. Mrs. Fairfax offered some to the mother dog, but though she managed to wag her tail weakly, she turned her head away from the bowl. Mrs. Fairfax shook her head sadly and went back to rubbing her gently with a fresh towel.

Linda kicked off what was left of her muddy shoes and sat down, cross-legged, on the floor, cradling the puppy in one hand. She filled the dropper with milk, let a single drop form on the tip, and then held it in front of the puppy's mouth.

"He won't touch it!" wailed Linda. The puppy squirmed helplessly in her hand and it suddenly mattered, more than anything she could remember, that this tiny creature should eat and live.

"Dip your finger in the milk and rub a little on his lips," said Mrs. Fairfax. Linda did as her mother suggested. For a moment the puppy lay still with the milk on his muzzle. Then the tip of his pink tongue reached out and tasted the milk. He suddenly lifted his head, which seemed much too big for him, and searched blindly in front of him.

"He wants more," Linda said softly. She put the dropper to the puppy's mouth again. This time, drop after drop of milk vanished behind the broad tongue.

"Not too much," cautioned Linda's mother. "You can give him more in a little while."

Mrs. Fairfax got to her feet. "I'll get my hot-water bottle and a cardboard box for him. We must keep him warm; I'm afraid his poor mother is in no condition to care for him now."

Linda heard her mother running up the creaking stairs; in a few minutes she was back, her eyes shining with excitement. Linda felt a quick stab of guilt; she hadn't seen her mother look anything but pale and worried for so long . . . .

Linda jumped quickly to her feet. Together, she and her mother lined a cardboard carton with an old flannel bathrobe, wrapped the warm hot-water bottle in a towel, and put the puppy beside it in the box. "He's lying awfully still," Linda said worriedly.

Her mother smiled. "He's warm and full of good milk, and he's asleep," she said. "Probably for the first time in his life."

Linda touched the top of the small black head with the tip of one finger. The puppy stirred gently in his sleep. Linda turned to look at the mother dog, who was barely breathing under the blanket which Mrs. Fairfax had put over her.

Linda's mother put her arm around her daughter's shoulder and held her for a moment. "Poor thing," Mrs. Fairfax said sadly. "I wish we knew where she came from and why she was out in the woods like that on her own. She's so terribly thin and tired . . . ."

She took a deep breath and started to bustle busily around the kitchen. "Put the puppy box over near the stove, Linda, and I'll start supper while you change your clothes."

Linda glanced down in astonishment at her torn and muddy skirt. She hadn't even noticed, and this

11

had been her favorite skirt. She rushed into dry clothes and hurried back to the bright kitchen.

"He's still sleeping," her mother reported with a happy smile. She glanced at her watch. "We'll feed him every hour through the night," she said. "If he doesn't get pneumonia from being born out there in those cold, wet woods, we might just be lucky enough to save him."

under 3 weeks

2 They built a fire in the fireplace in the living room and pulled the curtains across the windows. Outside, the wind howled and rattled the shutters in the dark, but in the small living room it was warm and bright.

Neither Linda nor her mother wanted to leave the puppy. They put the box at a safe distance from the crackling fire and took turns warming the hot-water bottle and offering the tiny puppy his milk from the medicine dropper every hour.

Midnight came. Linda put a fresh log on the fire and watched dreamily as the sparks swirled up and spun through the flames until they disappeared up the

13

chimney. Her mother made cocoa. Linda fed the puppy. When she put him back in his flannel nest, he stretched out his tiny paws and yawned with contentment. In just the few hours since Linda had found him, his narrow sides had filled out and he looked, they agreed, much less like a little rat and much more like a puppy.

Warm and dry and safe in the snug kitchen, the mother dog sank into a deep and peaceful sleep. About three o'clock, when the wind had died and everything was still, Linda tiptoed over to her and found that she was no longer breathing. Linda's throat ached with sorrow and pity. She knelt beside the motionless dog and pulled the blanket up over her head. "We'll take just as good care of your baby as we possibly can," she promised in a shaky whisper. "We won't let him die of hunger out in the cold, as somebody did to you. Not ever." She blinked the tears from her eyes and went to tell her mother.

The sun rose at last. Linda went to the window and pulled back the curtains, then caught her breath. The fields around the house were shimmering in a silver light streaked with splashes of gold from the rays of the early sun. For a moment Linda thought she was so sleepy that she was imagining things, and then she laughed out loud at herself. There had been frost dur-

ing the night, of course; living in the city as she always
had, she had never seen an early frosty morning before. In fact, when she thought of it, she had never
been up all night before, either.

She turned to call her mother to the window, then
stopped. Mrs. Fairfax had fallen asleep on the couch
by the fire. Moving on tiptoe, Linda got a quilt from
her room. She tucked it around her mother, quietly
added a fresh log to the fire, checked the sleeping
puppy, and went back to sit by the window.

She had fed the puppy twice more before her
mother stirred and sat up, looking flushed and guilty.
"Heavens! What time is it? Linda, you let me sleep!"
She swung her legs to the floor in sudden alarm. "The
puppy! He hasn't been fed. Is he all right?"

Linda grinned happily at her mother. "He's fine.
He's wonderful. He's fat and sound asleep. Come
look; he doesn't even look the same as he did last
night."

They bent over the box to admire the sleeping
puppy. In the bright light of morning they could see
that his black coat, short as it was, was beginning to
fluff out, and that there was a single streak of silver
gray behind each shoulder. "He looks as though he
were sprouting angel wings," Linda said with a gig-
gle.

15

"Then we'll have to call him Gabriel, of course," said her mother. They laughed together, enormously pleased with the success of their efforts.

Later that morning, Mrs. Fairfax stole precious minutes from her work to coax the battered old car into life and rattle her way down to the nearest drugstore, which was several miles away. While she was gone, Linda found a shovel in the sagging tool shed at the back of the house, and chose a spot beside the back garden where the ground was soft, near a small tree which her mother had said was a lilac. Linda started to dig.

It was harder work than she would have imagined. She still wasn't done by the time her mother returned, triumphantly bearing a baby bottle and a box of rubber nipples.

"These nipples are for premature babies," she told Linda. "They're smaller than the regular ones and they should be just perfect for the puppy. I got him some infant vitamins, too, to put in his milk. And I stopped by the library and found a wonderful book on dog care; there's a whole section in it on raising orphan puppies." She stopped to look at Linda wonderingly. "Whatever have you been doing to get yourself so hot and muddy?"

When Linda explained, her mother nodded, and went to find another shovel. Soon they had covered the blanket-wrapped body of the dog gently with earth.

They stood for a few minutes, catching their breath. Linda wiggled her sore fingers on the handle of the shovel. Three of her polished fingernails were broken off short, there was a splinter in the palm of one hand, and she didn't care.

"Lovely, to put her near the lilac," said Mrs. Fairfax. "Come on, darling, it's time we fed the young man again."

The puppy didn't like the hard rubber nipple. He kept pushing it away with his tiny paws and crying. "It's no use," Linda said despairingly. "He's going to starve himself to death."

"Here. Let me have him for a minute." Mrs. Fairfax sat down and cuddled the puppy against her wool sweater. She squeezed a drop of milk from the nipple and rubbed it against the puppy's stubbornly closed mouth. Then, very gently, she pressed two fingers on the sides of his jaws. The puppy opened his mouth just wide enough; Mrs. Fairfax slipped the milky tip of the nipple over his broad pink tongue. Linda found herself holding her breath.

Then, suddenly, the tiny jaws clamped shut and the

whole sunlit kitchen seemed to be filled with a wonderful sound—little sucking noises and the musical whisper of bubbles flowing through the milk in the bottle as the puppy drank.

Mrs. Fairfax laughed happily. "He's a regular tiger!" she exclaimed.

Linda let her breath out in an enormous, shaky sigh of relief. "How do you know so much about all this?" she said.

Mrs. Fairfax grinned at her daughter. "I raised a baby once myself, you know," she said.

She took the bottle gently from the puppy's mouth and held it upright. "Wow, he's taken half an ounce already! That's enough for one feeding. We don't want to make him sick." The puppy began to squirm and cry.

"I think he's still hungry," said Linda.

"I should imagine he's probably got a bubble," murmured her mother. She held the puppy upright and gently rubbed his back. The puppy gave one small hiccup and his head sagged to one side.

"He's dead!" Linda cried frantically. "What happened?"

"For goodness sakes, don't worry so much!" said her mother with an understanding smile. "He had a gas bubble, and now it's gone, and he's fallen asleep."

Gently she put the puppy in his flannel nest next to the freshly warmed hot-water bottle. "Two hours should do him now, I should think," she said, looking at the tiny black form with weary pleasure. "I'll see if I can get some work done. You'd better take a nap, Linda. I don't think either of us is going to get much sleep for the next few days."

3½ weeks

3 The puppy grew stronger by the hour. At the end of the first week Linda and her mother weighed him, with great ceremony, on the kitchen scale. "One and a quarter pounds," Mrs. Fairfax declared. "We'll keep a record every week from now on."

Linda sat in school trying to stay awake, took cat naps in the bus, but somehow managed to keep up with her homework well enough to get by. The girls in her class seemed more friendly, and when she explained sleepily one morning that she'd been up several times during the night with an orphan puppy, all of the girls nodded understandingly. Animals were a vital part of all their lives and the extra care they demanded was accepted as a matter of course.

Gabriel's eyes began to open eleven days later and his tiny ears, which had been lying close to his round little head, began to lift and stick out like scraps of paper—"just as though they'd been glued on wrong," commented Linda, admiring the puppy as she fed him that evening. "I wonder what breed of dog he is?"

"Several different kinds, I should imagine," said her mother. "But he's beautiful, anyway." The puppy's short black coat had grown thicker and longer, and showed traces of gray on the tips of the hair.

Thanksgiving came. The woods and fields were piled deep in heavy snow. The short winter days slipped by, and then it was Christmas. Linda had learned needlepoint at school, and had made her mother a bookmark with a design of flowers. She wrapped it carefully on Christmas Eve, looking at the small package doubtfully when she was done.

"It doesn't look like much," she said to Gabriel. "I hope she likes it."

By this time the puppy was in the middle of everything Linda did. He was lying on a rumpled sheet of Christmas wrapping paper, growling happily over a tangled roll of red ribbon. His tail had curled up over his back and was plumed with white and silver gray, and the markings on his head had changed to shades of black and silver, with pale circles around his dancing black eyes which made him look like a mischievous raccoon.

When Linda spoke to him he bounced across the room to her, yards of ribbon trailing behind him. "O.K., bright eyes," Linda said, laughing. "I know. Food. Just wait a minute."

She placed the wrapped present on her closet shelf, both to hide it from her mother and to keep it away from Gabriel's curious teeth and paws. She scooped the puppy up in her arms and buried her face in his deep, soft fur. "You're the best Christmas present either of us could have," she told the puppy as she carried him downstairs.

The kitchen smelled wonderful. Gabriel bounced around the floor, trying to reach the tabletop where a tray of cookies lay cooling. Linda mixed the puppy's supper of shredded wheat, hamburger, and milk, and she and her mother watched as he wolfed it down.

"He may look like a baby raccoon, but he eats like a

22

horse," said Linda's mother. "I wonder how big he's going to be."

It snowed on Christmas Eve, and all the next day. Linda's mother flushed with pleasure when she opened her present. "You've never made me anything before," she said. "This is the nicest Christmas present you've ever given me."

Linda looked at her mother thoughtfully. It was true. She had never given her mother anything she had made herself; Christmas had always been bright shops on Fifth Avenue, lots of gold paper and cardboard angels on department-store wrappings, and parties to go to and places to rush to and no time to sit in wintery sunlight and puzzle over a needlepoint flower petal.

There was an enormous box containing a pair of heavy corduroy slacks and wool-lined boots for Linda. "Time Gabriel was housebroken," her mother said with a laugh. "These are for taking him outside as soon as we clear a path through the snow!" There were other presents, too, but the best one of all was her own copy of the book on raising dogs.

Linda put it well out of Gabriel's reach, and gave him his presents: a bone made of rawhide and a ball with a bell in it. The puppy pounced on the ball, rolling it under the Christmas tree and around the living-room floor.

After the dinner dishes were done and Gabriel, full of his share of turkey, was asleep under the tree, Linda took the dog book and curled up on the couch by the fire.

"It says here that he has to have shots," she reported.

"There must be a vet somewhere in the area, with all the farms around here," said her mother. "I'll ask the next time I go marketing."

Gabriel raised his head. "You're a fuss and a bother and we love you dearly," said Linda. The puppy wagged his plumed tail and fell asleep again.

4 weeks

4 They were told of a vet who had an office not too many miles outside of town. It was the first trip for Gabriel in the car, and he enjoyed every minute, happily panting small clouds of steam onto the side window as he sat on Linda's lap.

"Might be part Husky," said the doctor as he examined the wiggling puppy. "Maybe a little bit of German Shepherd, too. But I'm sure of one thing. Whatever he is, you've got him in fine shape." He started to fill a syringe. "He'll need a series of three of these inoculations, then a booster shot in three months."

Linda glanced at Gabriel as Mrs. Fairfax held him on the examining table. His head cocked to one side, the puppy was watching the vet. Linda looked at the needle, looked back at the puppy, and fled. She couldn't bear to watch. She went out into the waiting room and concentrated fiercely on the doctor's bulletin board.

Cows for sale. Bulls. Horses and ponies. A tattered note about last fall's state fair, and a fresh white piece of paper with HELP! written across the top in red letters. Linda, curious, read the writing underneath.

"Help wanted for boarding kennels. Perfect after-school and weekend job for willing worker who likes dogs. Call after 5 o'clock."

Linda borrowed a pencil from her mother and made a note. Gabriel was getting expensive to keep; he was eating enormously, four times a day, and showed no signs of slowing down. Now there would be the cost of the shots, and through the open door to the examining room, she could hear her mother and the doctor discussing a schedule of worming for the puppy, and a vitamin-mineral powder to be given in his food. Linda smiled to herself as she tucked the scrap of paper into her pocket. It would be fun to be able to help.

She didn't mention her plan to her mother until she had called the number that evening. The phone was answered by a voice saying, "Wingover Kennels. Good evening."

Linda drew a deep, nervous breath. "Hello. My name is Linda Fairfax and I'm calling about the notice you had on Dr. Marshall's bulletin board. The one about needing help in your kennels."

When Linda hung up a few minutes later, she raced down the stairs and burst into the kitchen. "I've got an interview tomorrow afternoon for a job," she announced to her mother.

"One teaspoon of baking powder," said her mother. "Just a second. I don't want to lose count." She finished measuring and turned to give full attention to her daughter. "An interview? What kind of a job? Baby-sitting?"

"Dog-sitting," said Linda. "Well, sort of." And she told her mother about calling the boarding kennels. Gabriel capered into the kitchen in the middle of the conversation, dragging one of Linda's snow boots by the laces. Linda shrieked, the puppy barked, and though Mrs. Fairfax looked doubtful, in the confusion that followed she promised to let Linda go for the interview, at least.

"This isn't really necessary, you know," she told Linda as they drove along the snow-covered roads the next afternoon. "We're doing all right as we are. The publishers have seen the first part of the book and they were encouraging about it. It's been going really well these past few weeks." She glanced at the address on the seat beside her. "We can afford to keep Gabriel, honestly." She turned into the next driveway. "The kennels aren't very far from us," she said. "At least that's something."

She stopped the car by a long white building. "There's a sign saying 'office,'" she said. "I'll wait out here, Linda. I'm sure you'd rather go in alone."

Linda smiled at her gratefully. If she was old enough to be interviewed for her first job, she was old enough to tackle it alone, and she was glad her mother understood.

7 weeks

5 Linda liked her new job right from the beginning, though Katie and Paul Kent, who owned the kennels, were hesitant at first.

"We had really expected to have someone a little older," Katie had explained. "We have almost eighty dogs here and only a very few of them belong to us. The rest are boarders or show dogs which we condition and show for our clients. Of course, either Paul or I would be here to tell you what needs to be done; you wouldn't be handling the dogs themselves at first. Yours would be the dullest part, I'm afraid. Helping to clean the pens, keeping the water dishes clean and filled, scrubbing out feeding dishes—the chores to be done are endless in kennels this size. But we do need help badly, and you seem to be a calm and responsible kind of person."

"Please, just let me try," said Linda. "I'd like to help so much, I won't mind the dull bits, honestly."

With growing approval, Katie and Paul accepted Linda into the daily routine of the kennels. Linda loved to walk down the long, bright aisles with the stalls for the dogs on both sides, each of which opened to an outside run. At first many of the dogs looked alike to her, but as the days passed she learned to recognize them all as individuals. The twelve huge white and black Newfoundlands whose roar seemed to shake the foundations when strangers drove up to the kennels terrified Linda at first, until she discovered that each one had a personality of its own, and that every one was kind and gentle.

Not all of the dogs were friendly. Linda was told, right from the first day, never to touch any of the dogs without special instructions or permission from either Katie or Paul.

Every weekday afternoon the school bus dropped Linda off at the kennels. Most of the feeding was done in the morning with the help of a couple, Mr. and Mrs. Wilder, who came to the kennels until noon, but there were always a few dogs who needed a second

31

feeding, as well as aisles to be swept, stainless-steel feeding dishes to be scrubbed, water to change, and pens to be checked. Though the whole atmosphere of the kennels was calm and cheerful, it was a very busy place, and there was always something to be done.

Clients often came late in the afternoon to pick up their boarding dogs. No boarder left the kennels without a bath and a complete grooming, and, gradually, as the weeks spun into months, Linda helped more and more with the grooming. Working beside Katie and Paul, she learned how to brush and comb each breed, how to reassure a shy or frightened dog, and how to control a rambunctious puppy who thought that grooming should be a game.

She helped on weekends, as well. Sometimes she worked with Mr. and Mrs. Wilder, who stayed at the house near the kennels when Katie and Paul were away at a show. But non-showing weekends were best, because then Katie and Paul were there, schooling the show dogs and training young puppies, and had time to explain and answer Linda's questions.

The basic routine of the kennels never varied, but occasionally there were extra things to be done, such as when the veterinarian came to inoculate all the dogs in the kennels. At the end of one rainy Saturday, after helping to hold almost eighty dogs for their shots,

Linda collapsed, laughing, on the top of a crate in the grooming room. Katie was there, catching her breath, after wrestling with a half-grown Newfoundland puppy who was more interested in playing than in standing still for his shot.

"It really is funny to think how I couldn't even bear to watch when my puppy got his first shot last winter," said Linda. "Whoever could have guessed I'd be helping with eighty of them so soon!"

"You've learned a lot this winter," said Katie. "And you're doing a wonderful job. We're very glad you're here, Linda. Paul and I both hope you like it."

"I love it," Linda assured her. "I thought I'd be bored to death out here in the country. Instead, the days are too short, what with school, and helping you here, and taking care of my own puppy—"

"What kind did you say he was?" Katie started to tidy a tangle of leads and collars as they talked.

"Oh, he's just a mutt," said Linda. "But he's a wonderful dog, just the same. I've got him on the same food now that you feed your dogs, and he's growing like crazy, but he's still teething on every chair and table leg in the house."

"Ask the butcher at the market to give you a big, smooth knuckle bone and let the puppy chew on that. The next time you take him to a vet, ask him to check

33

the puppy's teeth. He may have one or two baby teeth that still haven't shed, and they may have to be pulled. He'll be much more comfortable once they're gone."

Katie was right; Gabriel did have two baby teeth that had not yet come out. The advantages of working at the kennels were enormous, Linda decided. She watched how Paul and Katie handled and lead-broke the puppies, and practiced the same way at home with Gabriel. She taught him to lie quietly on a table while he was being groomed, to be reasonably patient while she cut and filed his toenails.

"I hate doing this," Linda confessed to her mother one evening as she struggled with Gabriel, who was bored, and impatient for his evening walk. "But they're forever cutting the nails on all the dogs at the kennels to keep their feet from spreading out all wrong. It makes a lot of difference. I've seen some of the pets that come in for boarding or grooming whose nails haven't been cut for ages, and their feet look awful."

She gave Gabriel a hug and lifted him down from the table. The puppy capered wildly around the kitchen, begging to be taken out. Linda watched him for a few minutes, and then made a face.

"You sure are a funny-looking dog, in spite of anything I do," she told the happy puppy as she went to

34

get her jacket. "The more I groom you, and the more I learn about caring for you, the worse you look."

Gabriel no longer looked like a furry raccoon. His lovely shaded gray coat had changed. Now it was soft and close and the color of cream, except for the black spectacle markings around his dancing eyes, and his black ears and muzzle.

"Never mind," Linda said to him consolingly as they went outside. "Just because you look like a cross between a wolf and a sheep doesn't mean we don't love you just the same."

Spring came, then school was over for the summer. Mrs. Fairfax's book was going well, and she hummed while she scribbled notes in the margins of her growing manuscript. Linda swam in a nearby lake with her friends from school, picnicked, and went for long, happy walks with Gabriel, who was getting to be even more of a companion as he grew older and stronger.

She worked at the kennels in the mornings, now, as most of the work needed to be done before the afternoon sun got too hot. Only one small part of the kennels, a room off the end of one wing, was air-conditioned. Here they kept an Old English Sheepdog who suffered terribly in hot weather, an old but much-loved Boxer who had a bad heart, and one or two others who needed special care.

"Wouldn't it be much nicer to air-condition the whole place?" asked Linda one day as she pushed her long hair away from her hot face. "Wouldn't it be more comfortable for the dogs?"

Katie, who was carefully scissoring a white Poodle, stood back and looked at the dog with narrowed eyes. "Still a little too much over the ears, Muffin," she said to the dog, who wagged his tail in response. "No, Linda, we can keep the kennels cool by shading the runs and using heavy-duty exhaust fans. The dogs are smart. They keep still and quiet during the warmest part of the day. If you let them alone, and give them all the cool water they want, they do very well. Then it isn't such a terrible shock to them to go out into a blazing hot show ring on the weekends—that can really be hard on a dog used to air-conditioned kennels." She snipped a careful touch of hair from the Poodle's tail and scolded him fondly as he wagged it at her.

The summer fled by. The old Boxer died. A coughing virus was brought into the kennels by a new boarder; because Paul heard the dog's first few coughs and isolated him immediately, only four other dogs caught it, and prompt care prevented them from getting very sick.

A litter of thirteen Newfoundland puppies was

born and, because the mother had seen Linda often in the kennels, she was allowed to go into the room up at the house where the puppies were. Linda spoke gently to the mother and admired the wiggling mass of fat, nursing puppies, then stared in wonder at the equipment in the room. On a shelf were a small tank of oxygen, heat lamps, thermometers, piles of clean towels, and bottles of iodine and disinfectant. "It looks like a hospital," she said to Katie.

Katie was white with exhaustion, with deep shadows under her eyes, but she was smiling happily as they left the room.

"I suppose it does. Look like a hospital, I mean," she said vaguely. "But you need every bit of that equipment to whelp a litter of puppies. Lovely, lovely litter. We've been trying to breed this particular litter for three and a half years."

They walked quietly down the stairs and into the kitchen. "I am going to have a very strong cup of coffee and try to stay awake," said Katie. "Help yourself to a Coke if you'd like one, Linda."

"How many nights have you been up?" asked Linda curiously.

"Just three, so far," said Katie. "Paul and I will take turns for the next few nights. Cindy, the mother, is a funny dog. She was kicked once by a man when she was a puppy, and she's never really trusted men ever since. She'll let Paul come in to see her and to check the puppies, but she doesn't like him to handle them. It's all right, though. It evens out. The Bouvier des Flandres is due to whelp in ten days, and she doesn't even eat if Paul isn't around, so he gets to whelp her litter."

"I guess I don't really understand," said Linda. "Why can't they just have their puppies by themselves?"

Katie sat down with a steaming cup of coffee. "Because occasionally they need help," she said. "And when they do, they need it at once. Sometimes the mother is nervous and all she needs is someone there to reassure her. Sometimes when a puppy is born the mother doesn't pay enough attention to it, and if it doesn't have help to start breathing right away, it may never breathe at all. Four of those puppies upstairs needed a little oxygen to get them started, and now they are fine, strong puppies. One of them looks to be the best in the litter. It would have been a great loss, and inexcusable negligence, if that one had died just because no one was there to help when it was needed."

She got tiredly to her feet and started to warm a pan of milk. "Plus the fact," she added, stirring the milk, "that he may turn out to be worth anywhere up to fifteen hundred dollars, once he's grown up and in the show ring."

She smiled at Linda over her shoulder. "Raising good dogs is an expensive pastime," she said. "And it's a lot of work, a lot of trouble, a lot of grief, and a lot of fun." She turned off the stove and picked up the dish of milk. "Cindy's running a little bit of fever, and I'm trying to get all the liquids into her she'll take. Heaven help us all if her milk dries up—hand-raising thirteen Newfoundland puppies is an incredible job! But I've done it before." She glanced at her watch. "The vet is due to check her," she said. "She just started the fever, so we should be able to get her on antibiotics right away and keep everything going well, with a little bit of luck."

Linda waited by the door to watch for the vet. Luck, she decided, seemed to be more the result of care and hard work than just chance.

8 weeks

6 Linda ran across the field with Gabriel capering beside her. There had been a sharp frost during the night, and the morning smelled like fresh apple cider—bright, cool, and tangy.

A cock pheasant exploded from the long grass. Gabriel raced after him with one short, happy bark. Linda stopped to watch, knowing the chase would be brief and unsuccessful. The dog turned and flew back to Linda, bounding through the russet grass.

Linda smiled. He was almost a year old now, most of the time behaving with great dignity, but sometimes flinging himself back into puppy antics. His short, creamy coat was gone. Now it was full and shaded in grays and black, and a heavy ruff stood out like a silver cloud around his dark head. The pale markings around his dark, dancing eyes and the thin black spectacle markings made him look as though he were always laughing.

Linda knelt in the grass for a moment and hugged him. Whatever he was—part Husky, part wolf, or part anything else—he was a handsome dog and she was proud of him.

"Enough nonsense now, Gabriel," she told the panting dog. She took a lead from her pocket and slipped it over his head. "Time for company manners. You'll have the kennels in an uproar. We'll be there in a minute."

With Gabriel prancing by her side, Linda started down the hill to the long white buildings just showing through the trees.

Her mother had had to rush into New York that morning for an unexpected meeting with her editor; this meant leaving the house almost before daylight, and she wouldn't be back until late that afternoon. There was a teachers' meeting in another town that day, so there was no school, and Linda had promised happily to spend the day helping at the kennels.

Gabriel was the only problem. He was slightly

spoiled, Linda and her mother had to admit; he was not used to being left alone all day in the house. Hesitantly, Linda had asked Katie if she could bring him with her to the kennels for the day.

"Has he had all his shots?" Katie had asked, and Linda assured her he had. "Then bring him along, of course. He can have the run beside the two Kuvaszok."

Linda opened the door into the office. "Hi, I'm here," she called out, letting Gabriel walk into the room ahead of her.

Katie waved her hand in greeting, finished the note she was making in the appointment book, then turned to smile at Linda. The smile faded from her face and her eyes widened. She stood beside the desk as though she were frozen.

"Linda!" she said in a voice hardly more than a whisper. "*Where did you get that dog?*"

Linda stared, blinked, then glanced down at Gabriel, who was standing quietly at her side with his silvery plumed tail wagging gently and his black ears pricked. "Why, I told you, I found him in the woods. Ages ago. This is Gabriel."

Katie took a deep breath and walked over to the dog. She knelt beside him. Gabriel lifted one of his creamy paws and placed it gently on her hand. Linda

42

stood in stunned silence, completely bewildered, then dropped the lead and stepped back.

Katie ran her hands through the dog's deep coat, caught his head gently between her hands and looked at him with an expression on her face which Linda could not understand.

"Please tell me, is there something the matter?" asked Linda, finally breaking the silence.

The door into the kennels flew open before Katie could reply and Paul dashed into the room, waving a silver chain link collar in his hand. "The last of these good collars just broke, and—" He stopped, whirled, and then stood motionless, staring at Gabriel. "Katie, in the name of heaven, where did that dog come from?"

Linda was backed up now against the desk, her head spinning with confusion. Katie and Paul were both beside the dog, speaking to each other in low voices. Gabriel was the only one who didn't seem bothered or confused.

Paul looked up finally at Linda, a frown of concentration on his face. "Where . . ." he started.

"I found him. I've told you before. I found him in the woods." Linda felt as though she was going to cry. "I told you I'd found a dog, the vet said he was probably part Husky, we've had him a year. . . ." She burst

44

into tears, and rushed over to throw her arms around Gabriel. "I don't understand," she sobbed, burying her face in the dog's silver ruff. "What's the matter with him?"

Katie and Paul looked at each other. "We're sorry," Paul said, putting his hand gently on Linda's shoulder. "But he was quite a surprise to us. Come over here and sit down and let's talk for a minute."

Linda sniffed and found a tattered Kleenex in her pocket. She was careful to keep Gabriel close by her side as she went to perch uneasily on the edge of one of the office chairs.

"Now," said Katie gently. "Tell us again where you found that dog."

With a shaky sigh, Linda told her story of the discovery of the dying dog and her newborn puppy on that rainy evening, just a year ago. "But I don't see why he's such a surprise to you," she ended.

Gabriel, bored, had curled up and fallen asleep with his head on Linda's foot. Katie and Paul looked at him for a moment in silence.

"I don't think there's much doubt about it," said Paul, leaning forward and studying the dog again. "He's the image of old Mariner at this age."

"No question," agreed Katie. "Wow." She ran her hands through her hair. "Now what, Paul?"

Linda could feel her face flushing with anger. "I wish you would tell me what this is all about," she said stiffly.

"Just one minute, Linda," said Paul, "and I'll show you exactly what this is all about." He went to the storage closet, rummaged for a moment in a drawer, and brought out a framed photograph which he handed, in silence, to Linda.

The glass was a little dusty, and the photograph was slightly faded, but even so, Linda gave a gasp of astonishment. "Why, it's Gabriel!" she cried. "But—but it can't be! I don't understand." There was a red, white, and blue rosette beside the photograph in the frame. Linda could just make out the words "Best in Show" in dim gold letters on the ribbon, and the date—more than fourteen years ago.

"That dog in the photograph is Harborlight Master Mariner," said Katie. "One of the finest Kees ever bred in this country."

"What in the world is a Kees?" said Linda.

"That's a Kees," answered Paul, gesturing toward the sleeping dog at Linda's feet. "Kees—that's spelled K-e-e-s, but it's pronounced kays—is short for *Keeshond*. It's an old breed of Dutch origin. We used to breed and show them for a client, many years ago. She had some nice dogs, some of them were outstanding, but she had one really great one. Mariner." He paused and went over to look at the photograph Linda was still holding in her hand.

"He was owned by Mrs. Spencer Wentworth," said Katie, "and we showed him for her and won with him from one end of the country to the other. He was one of the first Keeshonden to win Best in Show in the United States." Katie's eyes grew dreamy as she remembered. "He was finally retired and he died a year or two later.

"We went on showing one of his daughters, a lovely little bitch called Harborlight's Heidi. After she finished her championship, Mrs. Wentworth took her home. A few days later, Heidi got out of the house somehow, ran down to the road, and was hit by a car. Her leg was badly broken in two places and there was some damage done to her shoulder. The vet was able to save her, but she was left with a limp, so her showing days were over. Mrs. Wentworth kept her as a pet."

Katie pulled a folder from the file drawer beside the desk and drew out a letter on pale blue paper. "We hadn't heard from Mrs. Wentworth for several years. When Mariner died, she seemed to lose interest in breeding and showing. All her good dogs were gone and she had nothing left but Heidi. Then, last June, this letter came from her. I'll read you the part that matters.

'A dear friend of mine, who now lives in Canada, recently imported a young Keeshond from England. She sent me a copy of his pedigree and this dog is heavily line bred to the foundation breeding behind my Master Mariner. I suddenly find that I cannot bear, after all these years, to let an opportunity like this go by. I have made arrangements to have my dear Heidi sent to Canada to be bred to this dog during her next season, which is due in about six weeks.' "

Katie slowly put the letter back into the file. "About three months later, Mrs. Wentworth called us late at night. Heidi had been sent to Canada, and she had been bred to the young English dog. When she was completely out of season, she was flown back to New York.

"Mrs. Wentworth sent her chauffeur to meet the plane and to bring Heidi home. He had a blowout on the state throughway on his way back, not far from here. The car went out of control and hit a tree. He was not hurt, but the back of the station wagon came open, the latch on the dog crate broke, and Heidi ran off into the woods."

"We went out that night, over to the throughway."

48

Paul picked up the story. "We called and searched for hours—but there wasn't a sign of her anywhere."

"It was awful." Katie shuddered. "The weather was getting cold, it rained and rained—it was a miserably wet fall—"

"I know," Linda said in a half-whisper. "And I know what you're trying to tell me. You're trying to say that it was Mrs. Wentworth's Heidi I found in the woods."

Katie shrugged her shoulders helplessly. "I don't know for sure, of course. But it certainly looks that way."

Linda put the photograph face down on the desk beside her. "But Gabriel is mine," she said firmly. "As far as I'm concerned, he's just a mutt, as he's always been, and *he is mine*." She snapped her fingers and the dog sprang instantly to his feet, ears pricked, and tail wagging. Linda took his lead tightly in her hand. "I think we'd better go home," she said, and started to move toward the door.

"Linda," Paul said gently. "You can't pretend we haven't told you all this. If you found a diamond ring in the woods, wouldn't you look for the owner and try to give it back?"

"But a ring isn't a living thing," Linda said fiercely. "Gabriel would have died if I hadn't found him in

49

time. I did find him, and I kept him alive, and I raised him and we love him. Nobody can know for sure if it was Mrs. Wentworth's dog that died in our house that night. It was just a poor, sick, starving gray dog that we tried to help." She ran out the door and shut it quickly behind her. With her dark hair flying, she ran with Gabriel to the path toward home.

Back in the office, Katie and Paul looked at each other in silence.

"We're going to have to let Mrs. Wentworth know about this," Paul said slowly.

"Are you sure we must?" Katie paced unhappily up and down the small office. "Of course we must. But there's no proof, no proof at all. . . ." She stopped and sat down. "Do you think Mrs. Wentworth will take the dog away from Linda?"

"What do you think?" said Paul. "No one, absolutely no one, says 'no' to Mrs. Wentworth. Especially if she wants anything the way she's going to want that dog."

9 weeks

7 Two days later, Mrs. Wentworth called. Linda didn't answer the telephone; she was feeding Gabriel. Her mother came into the kitchen a few minutes later with a strange look on her face. "Mrs. Wentworth is coming to see Gabriel on Sunday afternoon," she said.

"Oh." Linda watched Gabriel polish the bottom of his dish and finish a stray crumb of kibble he found under the rim. "I wonder if I should give him more to eat." She picked up the dish and carried it to the sink. "All right. Sunday." She let the hot water run until the steam drifted around her face. "Maybe we'll be lucky enough to have a blizzard by Sunday, and all the roads will be closed."

But it didn't snow. The weather stayed bright and warm with brilliant, sunny skies that were almost unbearable to Linda in their cheerfulness. The days seemed long and empty; she couldn't bear to go back to the kennels. She knew she was wrong, but at the same time she couldn't help feeling that she and Gabriel had been betrayed by Katie and Paul.

She took Gabriel for long walks and read endlessly, then couldn't remember the name of a single book she'd been reading.

Linda had decided to let Gabriel get as dirty, muddy, and matted as he could for Mrs. Wentworth's visit, but late Saturday evening, she suddenly changed her mind. In a frenzy of determination, she started to work on the dog's heavy coat. With a metal-bristled brush and a comb she went over every inch of the dog while he alternately looked bored or went to sleep. She ended up by powdering the white petticoats on his hindquarters, and his light silver ruff, with the last bit of her mother's bath powder. Gabriel sneezed reproachfully as she brushed it out, but his light shadings were left bright and clean. The kitchen smelled like a hothouse garden as the perfumed powder drifted over the floor.

Linda's mother, coming in to pour herself a fresh cup of coffee, blinked, sneezed, and threw her hands in the air. "Couldn't you have used something just a little less expensive?" she mourned, picking up the empty box.

"I'm sorry." Linda sat back on her heels, the brush in her hand. "I really didn't realize this was the last of your good stuff. Katie and Paul use talcum powder when they brush out the show dogs, and this was the only powder I could find."

Gabriel stood up and shook himself. Clouds of scented powder swirled around the kitchen. "Whew!" Mrs. Fairfax opened the back door. "Go on outside, Gabriel, and run around for a minute. We can air out the kitchen at the same time."

Linda and her mother laughed as the dog bounded out the door and they started to sweep up the flying powder. It felt good to laugh, even for a short while, but Linda wondered later, standing at the door whistling for Gabriel, whether there would be much laughter after Mrs. Wentworth's visit the next day.

She and her mother had discussed the problem over and over during the past few days. Linda had told her mother about the morning at the kennels, and what Katie and Paul had said. They had wondered and worried until finally Mrs. Fairfax had said, "This is all very dramatic, Linda, and quite a complicated situation, but we don't have to give the dog up without

53

a legal fight. There are laws about possession. And I think the most important thing to remember is that, no matter how much Gabriel may look like Mrs. Wentworth's old dog, it may be nothing more than coincidence. There is no proof, and without proof, no one can take the dog from us."

But in spite of her mother's encouraging words, Linda felt a miserable lump in her stomach. From the little she had heard that morning at Katie and Paul's, Mrs. Wentworth sounded like a terribly determined kind of person.

At exactly 3:30 on Sunday afternoon, a long black car drifted to a stop in front of the house. Kneeling on the window seat, peeking nervously through the living-room window, Linda saw a uniformed chauffeur move swiftly to the door of the car and open it. There was a pause, then the chauffeur offered his arm and a tall woman in a fur coat stepped out onto the stony driveway.

Although Linda heard her mother's voice introducing herself and asking Mrs. Wentworth to come in, she waited until she heard the sound of the front door closing before she forced herself to stand up. Moving slowly but with great dignity, with the help of a cane, Mrs. Wentworth came into the living room.

"Mrs. Wentworth, I'd like you to meet my daughter, Linda—"

Introductions were made, the fur coat was carefully hung in a closet, and Mrs. Wentworth was helped to the armchair near the crackling fire. There was a long, stiff silence. Linda and Mrs. Wentworth faced each other across the living room.

"Now, my child." Mrs. Wentworth's eyes glittered as sharply as the heavy rings on her hands, and she spoke in a surprisingly commanding voice. "Where is the dog?"

Without a word, Linda turned and went to the kitchen where she had put Gabriel to wait. He rose to his feet, yawned, stretched, and trotted with interest into the living room. He stopped for a moment, confused, as he became aware of the strange silence.

"His name is Gabriel," said Linda.

"Gabriel." Mrs. Wentworth spoke his name gently. The dog's head went up, his ears pricked, and his tightly curled tail began to move uncertainly. He took two steps forward onto the bright braided rug in the center of the room, and stopped again.

"Gabriel." Mrs. Wentworth held out her hand to the dog. He moved over to her, sat in front of her, and lifted his paw and rested it lightly on Mrs. Wentworth's knee.

There was a long interval of absolute silence. The fire snapped and sparked in the fireplace. Mrs. Fairfax sat motionless on the couch, and Linda, discovering with astonishment that her hands were sweaty, jammed them into the pockets of her slacks.

"Tell me, child," said Mrs. Wentworth slowly. "Tell me again where you found this dog."

Linda told the story again in short, quick sentences. There was a pause. Mrs. Wentworth fumbled in her black handbag and touched a handkerchief to her eyes. Gabriel, feeling he had been dismissed, came over to lie at Linda's feet.

"You know, of course, what happened." Mrs. Wentworth sat up firmly in the deep armchair. "Katie said she told you the story of my sending Heidi to be bred, and about the accident and the loss of the dog while she was being shipped back home. There is no doubt, no doubt at all, that this is her puppy."

"There must be doubt," Mrs. Fairfax said gently. "We know how you feel, Mrs. Wentworth, and we know how much you would like Gabriel to be the dog you're looking for, but there is no way of proving this."

"Proof?" Mrs. Wentworth's voice rose and tapped the floor with her black cane. "Why, just look at that dog. He's the image of his grandfather! He is the dog I have been waiting for, and trying to breed, for twenty years! He is magnificent, magnificent! He is the result of generations of line breeding, the finest bloodlines of two countries, a superb specimen of his breed, and you want me just to leave him here, buried in the country as a child's pet. . . ."

She broke off and looked at Linda with her direct, sharp eyes. "Child," she said, "come here." Almost in a trance, Linda went over to her.

"I am a very old lady," said Mrs. Wentworth in a softer voice. "I have been many places and seen many things, but one of the things that meant most to me in all those happy years was the raising and showing of my beautiful Kees. I believed this part of my life was over; when my dear Mariner died, I thought there would never be another dog to take his place. Now, here is Gabriel, like a ghost from the past, to give me one last chance. His heritage is the show ring, Linda. You cannot hide anything this beautiful, the result of so many, many years of planning and breeding and caring—it isn't right." She took one of Linda's hands between her own.

"You're a bright young thing. You know as well as I do there may well be proof that the dog you found dying in the woods was my Heidi." She paused for a moment. "Where did you bury her, Linda?"

Linda glanced frantically at her mother, but her mother was looking puzzled; she did not understand. Linda felt a cold wet nose poking gently at her hand. Gabriel, worried by the tension in the room, had come over to stand at Linda's side. She looked down at him and stroked the top of his dark head.

"It isn't fair," whispered Linda.

"I know." Mrs. Wentworth nodded a little sadly.

"Maybe the vet didn't keep Heidi's x-rays," said Linda.

"He has them," Mrs. Wentworth answered.

Mrs. Fairfax looked up in sudden shocked understanding. The broken leg which had healed imperfectly—all that was needed to prove that Gabriel belonged to Mrs. Wentworth was the skeleton of the dog they had buried. If it had a healed broken leg which matched the x-rays, Gabriel was indeed Heidi's puppy.

Mrs. Fairfax started to speak, then shut her lips in a firm line. This was Linda's battle which she must fight out with herself, if she possibly could. She tried to give her daughter an encouraging smile, but she felt too close to tears herself to be able to do it.

"I'll get my coat and show you," said Linda in a

shaky voice, after a long and miserable silence. "Maybe it isn't the right dog at all."

The chauffeur took the shovel from Linda's numb hand and started to dig, very gently and with great care, at the spot Linda showed him without speaking. Linda called Gabriel to her and they walked across the adjoining field to the top of the hill, where they could see the long white buildings of the kennels in the valley below. It was late afternoon and the crisp air was very still. Gabriel pricked his ears and listened to the faint sound of a single dog barking from far away.

Linda waited. She heard the sound of murmuring voices, the trunk of a car being closed, then car doors, and the sound of an engine which grew fainter and then died away into the distance. Linda shivered. It was getting cold and dark. She and Gabriel started back to the glow of the lights in the windows of the house.

10 weeks

8 The next week seemed endless as they waited to hear from Mrs. Wentworth. Gabriel felt the worry in the house and followed Linda quietly whenever she was home from school, curling up and resting his head on her foot while she did her homework.

Friday came. The school bus dropped Linda off at her driveway. "Hi, Mom, I'm home!" she called out as she tossed her books onto the table in the hall and took off her jacket. "I'm going to change and take Gabriel for a walk—"

She heard the sound of the car then, as it came to a

stop by the front steps. And she knew, with a miserable sick feeling in her stomach even before she went to the door, that it must be Mrs. Wentworth.

Seated once more in the living room with Mrs. Fairfax and Linda watching her in silence, Mrs. Wentworth drew three x-rays from their envelopes.

"These are very clear," said Mrs. Wentworth. She held one x-ray out to Linda, who took it reluctantly. "This first plate is dated on the lower left corner, as you can see, Linda. It is one taken when my Heidi was hit by the car. If you hold it up to the light, you can see that the long bone has been broken in two places, and that there's a chip out of her shoulder blade."

Linda held the x-ray up to the light and nodded wordlessly. She could see the breaks clearly. She handed the plate to her mother.

"This was taken several weeks later, after the breaks had healed." Linda nodded again. "And this—" Mrs. Wentworth looked at Linda sympathetically as she held out the last plate. "This is an x-ray, taken just three days ago, of the bones of Gabriel's mother."

Mrs. Wentworth leaned back in the chair. "There are more x-rays from other angles. Dr. Thoranson is a very thorough man. There is no doubt whatsoever that they are all of the same dog, and he is willing to swear this in court, if necessary."

Mrs. Fairfax flushed angrily, but Mrs. Wentworth raised her thin hand in a gentle gesture.

"Please, Mrs. Fairfax, I did not mean that as a threat. I said it only to stress the fact that truly there can be no question, whatsoever, that Gabriel is Heidi's son."

Linda sat down abruptly on a stool near the fireplace and stared in silence at the flames. Mrs. Wentworth slid the x-rays back into their envelopes and dropped them on the coffee table with a dismissing gesture.

"So now what are we to do about Gabriel?" Mrs. Wentworth folded her hands and her rings sparkled in the firelight. "I could offer you money for the dog, of course. Have you any idea what he is worth?"

"It makes no difference," Mrs. Fairfax said in a firm voice.

"No, I did not imagine it would." Mrs. Wentworth smiled. "I have a check in my purse, but I was very much afraid that it would not get me the dog."

Gabriel came prancing into the room just then, and rushed over to Linda. She stroked his smooth head absently, her eyes still on Mrs. Wentworth.

Mrs. Wentworth sighed heavily and suddenly looked very pale and tired. She leaned her head back against the chair and closed her eyes for a moment.

"Let me get you some tea," murmured Linda's mother, swiftly rising to her feet and hurrying to the kitchen.

The fire flickered and snapped. Gabriel got up and went over to Mrs. Wentworth and put his paw gently on her knee. Traitor! thought Linda savagely to herself. She put her chin on her knees and scowled at the fire.

The tea helped. A little color came back into Mrs. Wentworth's cheeks. She put her teacup back onto its saucer with a determined little click and reached out both her hands to Linda.

"I will not go to court, and I will not take the dog away from you." Linda rose to her feet with a surge of joy. "I want you to give him to me, instead."

"*What?*" cried Linda.

"He would not go entirely away from you," Mrs. Wentworth went on quietly. "Katie and Paul have been my handlers for years. The dog would go to their kennels and then they would show him when he is ready." She smiled at Gabriel, who was panting heavily from the heat of the fire but not wanting to leave to find a cooler spot. "You could see Gabriel every day, and help get him ready, and be part of everything this dog was meant to be. Think about it a little, Linda. Think of Gabriel. Think of the years of planning and caring and hoping—and disappointments, too, of course—and then finding one last chance again, after so many, many years. . . ."

Her voice trailed off into silence. She dropped her hands into her lap again. Gabriel left to find his favorite cool spot on the bare floor near the door.

Linda watched the steam curling from the spout of the teapot in silence, then pushed her hair away from her face impatiently. "This whole thing is absolutely ghastly," she said. "Mother, what do you think?"

Mrs. Fairfax shook her head. "I think that this is a decision you must make yourself, Linda."

Linda turned to look at Gabriel. It had been almost a year since she had slammed out the front door as a silly, whining brat, and found Gabriel, who had changed a lot of things. Now she knew, with a hollow, sinking feeling, that he was about to change everything again.

"All right, Mrs. Wentworth," she broke the silence at last. "I think I've known all along, ever since the day Katie and Paul first saw him, that this had to happen."

She called to Gabriel, who charged across the braided rug and stood in front of her with his black ears pricked and his pink tongue lolling. She knelt and buried her face in his heavy silver ruff.

"I don't know if you can truly understand how happy you have made me," said Mrs. Wentworth. There were tears in her eyes. She accepted a second cup of tea from Mrs. Fairfax and beamed down at Linda, her thin face now sparkling with excitement. "We'll have a marvelous time," she said. "We'll go to all the shows together, Linda . . ." She smiled at her own enthusiasm. "Of course, we must not be carried away by optimism. The dog is still quite young. He will not be at his very best until he is three years old, or more. But that is a long time to wait. Too long. Far, far too long."

She stood up stiffly and swayed for a moment, holding onto the side of the chair. "Too much excitement in one day for an old lady, I'm afraid," she said to Mrs. Fairfax. "If you wouldn't mind telling Walter, my dear, that I must leave. . . ."

The chauffeur helped her gently down the front steps. The long black car swept silently down the drive and out of sight. Linda fumbled blindly in the pocket of her jacket for Gabriel's lead. "He never got his afternoon walk," she said, desperately trying not to cry. "Come on, Gabriel." She ran outside with the dog bounding at her side.

11 weeks

9 Linda could not bear to take Gabriel to the kennels herself. Her mother took him over the next morning while Linda was in school. The small house seemed unbearably empty. Every evening, just at five o'clock, Linda would begin to fidget restlessly with her homework and wander uneasily around the house until she would realize what the trouble was—it was the time she always fed Gabriel and let him out for a run.

Curled up on the couch after dinner trying to concentrate on her books, time after time Linda would jump to her feet, sure she had heard Gabriel scratching at the back door and crying to come in.

"Why don't you go to see him?" Mrs. Fairfax suggested gently one morning. "He's not dead, you know. He's perfectly fine and waiting for you just over the hill. Katie called last night, just after you'd gone to bed. Gabriel has settled in very well and they all miss you. And they need to know whether or not you're planning to come back to work at the kennels. If you're not, you must let them know so they can find someone else."

"O.K." Linda sighed and picked up her books. "I guess seeing him there can't be much worse than missing him like this. Though I'm not really sure."

It felt strange to be getting off the school bus at the kennels again that afternoon. Linda hesitated at the door, suddenly ready to change her mind and go home. But before she had the chance, Katie opened the door and greeted her enthusiastically. "It's so nice to have you back!" she said.

And it was nice to be back, thought Linda, hearing the thundering roar of greeting from the Newfoundlands and the higher, happy barks of the other dogs as she and Katie went out into the fenced yard that enclosed the outside runs.

"QUIET!" shouted Katie, and all the dogs stopped barking at once but continued to wag their tails gaily. They put their paws up on the sides of their runs as

68

she and Linda walked by, speaking to each of them by name.

Finally Linda could wait no longer. "Please," she said, "where is Gabriel? Is he all right? I don't see him anywhere."

"He's on the other side, with the show dogs," said Katie with a smile. "But brace yourself. He looks a little strange."

"Strange? He looks awful!" wailed Linda as they stopped outside Gabriel's run. "What have you done to him?"

"His coat was a little dry from living indoors, so we've put a special oily dressing on it," said Katie, opening the gate. "Look out, that stuff is black and greasy. It will get all over you!"

But Linda didn't care. She knelt as Gabriel flung himself through the gate and into her arms.

After thoroughly covering Linda's white sweater with smears of black dressing, Gabriel whirled and pounced on Katie. Linda felt a stab of jealousy as she watched Katie pick up an old tennis ball and throw it across the yard. Gabriel tore after it and then frisked in a circle, the ball in his mouth and his dark eyes sparkling with mischief.

"He looks awfully happy," said Linda in a low voice. "I thought—I was *sure* he'd miss me more."

"Of course he misses you," said Katie. "Just as you miss him. But it's part of our job to make him happy here. Paul and I spend a lot of time with the dogs— you know that, you've seen us—getting them used to the routine of the kennels, getting them settled and responding to us. How well do you think a dog would show for us if he didn't like us or trust us?"

Gabriel trotted over to Linda, flung the tennis ball at her feet, and rolled over on his back, waving his paws in the air. Linda knelt to rub his stomach. "I know this must sound like kind of a silly question," she said, "but do they ever forget?"

Katie shook her head firmly. "Never. Gabriel will love you forever, just as he did two weeks ago, and just as he does today. And I'll tell you something else. It doesn't matter whose name is on the registration certificate. Gabriel can't read, and even if he could, he wouldn't care. As far as he's concerned, he's your dog, and he always will be."

Linda stood up and sighed. Gabriel gave her a reproachful look, got to his feet, and trotted off to touch noses with the Irish Wolfhound in a nearby run.

"Gabriel!" At Katie's command, the dog came flying back across the yard and trotted cheerfully into his own run at a wave of Katie's hand. She latched the gate and turned to Linda. "I promise you he's all right," said Katie, "but I know this is a difficult time for you. Maybe—what do you think? Would another puppy help?"

"No, thank you," Linda said. "It wouldn't be the same. I guess I'd rather share the little bit I can here with Gabriel."

The first few days were hard, expecially in the late afternoon when it was time for Linda to go home. At the end of each afternoon, she helped let the dogs in from their runs for the night. She watched as they pattered up the ramps with their tails wagging and flopped down contentedly in their pens as the doors were shut. Some had treasured old blankets to lie on, others had favorite toys. Gabriel had his own enormous rawhide bone and his ball with the bell in it, and when Linda went to say good night to him, he would be either rolling the ball across the floor or lying on his back with the bone between his paws, gnawing happily on one knobby end.

"So I guess it's pretty silly to worry about him," Linda finally had to admit to her mother after a week had passed. "He looked sort of puzzled the first few evenings I left him there, but he seems to understand now that I'll be back."

A few days later Linda helped to wash some of the

71

dressing out of Gabriel's coat, and Katie and Paul started taking the delighted dog with them every time they went to do an errand in town. Paul took him to the post office and to the railroad station; one busy Saturday morning, Katie drove to the nearest city and spent an hour walking the dog through the crowded streets. She came back beaming with satisfaction.

"He's got nerves of steel," she reported. "Nothing bothers him. He was a little astonished at first by all the people and traffic, but it didn't take him long to decide there was nothing to worry about.

"We're trying to get him used to as many strange sights and sounds as we can," Katie explained to Linda as she patted Gabriel and put him back in his run. "He's led a very sheltered life out here, and the noise and confusion of a dog show can be a terrible shock to an inexperienced dog if he hasn't had any preparation."

Katie and Paul taught him to trot beside them without tugging at the lead and to stand squarely with his tail curled over his back and his ears pricked. Every knowledgeable visitor to the kennels was asked to touch the dog and run their hands over him. This was often difficult for a dog to accept, Paul told Linda. Many dogs disliked being handled by strangers, but show dogs must learn to accept this as part of being judged in the show ring.

Gabriel loved all the extra attention. Whenever strangers came to the kennels he began dancing in his run, hoping it was time for another practice session. He went out every day either with Katie or Paul for two miles of roadwork, or for a romp with Linda in the wide, tightly fenced field behind the kennels.

Linda came into the kennels one afternoon, gasping for breath, with Gabriel capering joyfully beside her. "I can't wear him out," she said to Katie. "Why does he have to be so fit just to trot around a show ring?"

Katie smiled. "You can't hide an unfit dog under a pretty coat," she said. "Just look at him, Linda. He moves with a drive he never had before. He's up on his toes, he feels so well that he sparkles all over, and he's eating almost twice as much as he did when he first came in—and every bit of it is going into good hard muscle. Conditioning a show dog is as important as his schooling."

Mrs. Wentworth had come several times to see Gabriel and one afternoon, when Linda got off the school bus, she saw the familiar long black car up at the Kents' house. Mrs. Wilder was at the kennels and told Linda that Katie had left a message—would Linda please come up to the house? Linda ran quickly along the driveway, wondering if there was something wrong, but found Katie and Paul and Mrs. Wentworth pouring over albums of clippings and photographs. Pedigree forms were scattered over every table in the living room.

"Hi!" said Katie. "We thought you'd like to see all of this!" Linda watched and listened as the pages of the albums were turned.

"This is old Garry. Paul, remember when you won the Group with him at Devon in the thunderstorm? What a splendid mover he was." Mrs. Wentworth smiled at Linda. "He was Mariner's sire, and Heidi's grandsire on her dam's side as well." Photographs of Kees, talk of bloodlines and pedigrees, line breeding, outcrossing—Linda's head whirled as she tried to remember it all.

Finally the last album was shut and Mrs. Wentworth turned again to Linda. "Thirty years of Kees, my dear. Thirty years of breeding and showing Harborlight Kees. That's a lot of responsibility for one young dog to carry. What do you think now, Katie? Paul? Do you still think that Gabriel is the one we've been waiting and hoping for?"

Linda held her breath as she waited for the answer. After all, if Katie and Paul decided that Gabriel was not what they'd hoped or expected, she knew they would say so, and she could take Gabriel home.

Linda fidgeted uneasily. Much as she missed having Gabriel with her at home, she realized how much she had started to enjoy working with him at the kennels. It was exciting to think of him going out with the other show dogs, and though the names on the pedigrees and the numberless photographs still didn't mean much to her, she was beginning to understand what Gabriel represented, and she was proud of him.

"He's still very young," Paul said cautiously. "But, in time—"

Mrs. Wentworth nodded.

"He shows a lot of promise," said Katie.

"Exactly." Mrs. Wentworth nodded again, looking pleased.

Linda was bewildered and almost angry. "Don't you like him? Don't you think he's wonderful any more?"

Mrs. Wentworth smiled. "There is a saying about race horses that is just as applicable to show dogs, Linda. 'The trees go by very fast when you're galloping alone.' What Katie and Paul just said is praise enough. The dog is worthy of being shown. Now we must see what he can do in competition."

"Ten days," said Paul. "We have him entered in his first two shows the weekend after next."

All of the eight dogs entered had to be bathed during the week before the shows. Linda helped with Gabriel, who emerged from his bath free of the coat dressing at last. Four hours later Katie put down her brush. "There," she said. "He's done for now."

Linda stretched her aching arms, put down the brush she'd been using, and stepped back from the grooming table as Katie spoke to Gabriel. He had been lying on his side, half-asleep, enjoying all the attention, but at Katie's command he jumped to his feet, shook himself, and stood waiting.

"Wow," breathed Linda. The dog's magnificent coat stood out in a cloud of shaded silvers and black. Linda touched the top of his head almost shyly.

Katie laughed as she lifted the dog off the crate. "He's still the same dear Gabriel underneath," she said. "You can put him away, Linda. We'll do the two Newfoundlands tomorrow."

4½ months

10

"Here we are." Mrs. Wentworth glanced at the judging program in her hand. "Keeshonden, ring 9."

Completely bewildered, Linda just nodded without saying anything. There were tents and rows of rings marked off by low wooden fences, people everywhere, and dogs of all possible descriptions being walked, groomed, hurried to classes, lying solemnly in crates under the tents, or being brushed or scissored on grooming tables.

She followed Mrs. Wentworth's slow procession down the grassy stretch between the rows of rings, helped to find her a chair, and sat cross-legged on the grass beside her. There were five small black dogs with white markings in the ring in front of them and Linda stared at them blankly. They all looked exactly alike to her.

"Where is Gabriel?" she asked impatiently. "Why can't we go to see him?"

"He'll be in the handlers' tent," said Mrs. Wentworth. "Katie and Paul will have all their dogs together in one spot over in that tent, across the way. They will be getting Gabriel ready now. Kees are due in this ring as soon as these Boston Terriers are done. And you can't go anywhere near Gabriel until the judging is over.

"In fact," Mrs. Wentworth continued cheerfully, "you will have to move well away from the ringside before his class. My being here won't distract him because he does not know me well enough for it to matter, but he must not see you or hear your voice. All his attention must be on Katie or Paul, whoever is handling him today."

Linda's heart gave a jump of excitement as she saw a Keeshond standing near the ring gate. "There he is," she whispered.

"I doubt it," Mrs. Wentworth said comfortably. "Katie and Paul have more sense than to bring him out so soon." Linda subsided as she looked at the dog more carefully. Of course it wasn't Gabriel. But it was hard to realize, since Gabriel was the only Keeshond she had ever seen, that there were twenty-three of them entered here today.

The judging of the Bostons was finished. The ring was cleared.

"Now what happens?" asked Linda.

"The Kees will be next," said Mrs. Wentworth. "The five dog classes will be held first—technically, the word 'dog' means the male. Gabriel is entered in the last of these classes, the Open class, in which you can show male Kees of any age, as long as they are at least six months old.

"The five winners of these classes then will compete for Winners Dog, and the winner of this class receives points toward his championship. The number of points depends on the number of dogs he has beaten at this particular show, and it takes fifteen points all together to make a dog a Champion of Record.

"Then the same classes are held for the bitches, or females, and the Winners Dog and Winners Bitch automatically become eligible to compete in the next class, which is Best of Breed. Except for the two Winners, this class is open only to dogs and bitches which have already completed their championships in past shows.

81

"The winner of this class is Best of Breed—in other words, in the opinion of the judge, the best Keeshond in the show today."

Linda made a face. "It sounds pretty complicated," she said. "Is that the end?"

Mrs. Wentworth shook her head with an understanding smile. "No, not yet," she said. "Next the Winners Dog and Winners Bitch compete against each other for Best of Winners.

"After that, the judge chooses the Best Opposite Sex to Best of Breed. For instance, if the Best of Breed winner is a male, the judge will select the best bitch for Best Opposite.

"And that *is* the end."

Linda sighed. "I hope I can remember all that." She scrambled to her feet. "Look, look!" Two Kees puppies were gamboling in the ring with their handlers and the Keeshond judging was about to begin.

The puppies did not gait very well. They would trot only a few steps before either sitting down or jumping up on their handlers, trying to play. But the handlers and the judge were not bothered by the puppies' antics.

"The judge makes allowances," Mrs. Wentworth explained, "because the puppies are so young. It would be unreasonable to expect them to behave like

82

seasoned campaigners. All of this is wonderful experience for them."

Linda nodded. The judge awarded the ribbons and the puppies left the ring. Older Kees came in. Linda tried to concentrate on the classes, but she found it impossible.

Finally, Mrs. Wentworth clasped her hands tightly on the dog show catalogue in her lap. "You'll have to move now, Linda," she said. "Gabriel's class is next."

Standing on tiptoe behind the other spectators, Linda watched with growing excitement as the ring filled with Kees. For one breathless moment, she could not find Gabriel. She was suddenly sure that either she was so stupid she couldn't even recognize her own dog, or Katie and Paul had forgotten to bring him.

Then she laughed with relief. Of course Gabriel was there. Katie was with him, and they were standing quietly at the far corner of the ring. Linda's heart sank. Gabriel looked paralyzed with bewilderment. His black ears were flat back against his head and his silver-plumed tail, which Linda had never seen carried any way but up over his back, was drooping in a peculiar half-hearted curl.

Linda was frantic. Why didn't Katie do something? Didn't she realize how awful he looked?

After a few moments, Gabriel glanced up at Katie

and moved his tail a little. She spoke softly to the bewildered dog. He wagged his tail again. Katie offered him a tidbit which he sniffed uncertainly. Then she patted him cheerfully. The dog's ears came up and he took one step forward. As he did, his tail swept up over his back again. Another tidbit, more encouraging words from Katie, and Gabriel shook himself as though he were waking up from a bad dream. He turned his head and looked around him. Gradually, moment by moment, his assurance grew. Encouraged by Katie's quiet voice, reassured by her firm hand on his lead, Gabriel lost his worried, frozen look and even bounced happily for a step or two as Katie moved him into the line of other dogs.

The judge motioned the handlers to take their dogs around the ring in single file. Gabriel trotted briskly along beside Katie, wagged his tail with interest as the judge came over to examine him, and generally behaved as though he'd been a show dog all his life. The judge motioned to Katie, who led Gabriel to the first-place marker at the side of the ring.

"A good dog, well schooled and well handled," said Mrs. Wentworth with enormous satisfaction as Linda rushed up to her.

Katie tucked the blue ribbon into her pocket and waited in the ring with Gabriel.

"Now can we go to see him?" asked Linda, wild with excitement and impatience.

"Not yet, child," Mrs. Wentworth said calmly. "Gabriel still must not see you. If you would help me move my chair back into the shade, we can watch the rest of the judging together."

Gabriel and Katie were joined in the ring by the dogs Linda recognized as the winners of the previous classes. The five dogs were gaited and gone over again by the judge, and Katie left the ring with a purple ribbon in her hand.

"That gives him Winners Dog," said Mrs. Wentworth. "Lovely. He's won his first points toward his championship. What a nice beginning."

"Now?" asked Linda.

"Not yet, child," Mrs. Wentworth said again.

They watched impatiently as the five bitch classes were held. Eventually, the Winners Bitch ribbon was awarded and Mrs. Wentworth straightened her shoulders with renewed excitement. Seven Kees came into the ring, then Gabriel and the Winners Bitch, and the class began.

It seemed to drag on endlessly. Mrs. Wentworth frowned. "This is an unusually difficult class to judge today," she said to Linda. "There are some exceptionally fine champions here. The judge is also considering

Gabriel, I believe. But one can hardly hope to go all the way to Best of Breed the first time out—the dog has already done more than well enough. I just hope he doesn't tire."

But Gabriel was tired. Linda could tell. His sparkle of the first two classes was gone, and it was almost a relief instead of the disappointment she had expected to feel when the Best of Breed dog was chosen—one of the older champions—and all the dogs finally left the ring.

"But if Gabriel wasn't Best of Breed, what was the blue and white striped ribbon the judge gave Katie before all the classes ended?" asked Linda as she and Mrs. Wentworth made their way slowly toward the handlers' tent at last.

"Best of Winners," said Mrs. Wentworth. She looked tired but very pleased. "Gabriel has done exceptionally well, expecially for a young dog at his first show."

Linda dodged a friendly German Shepherd who was dragging his handler around the announcer's stand, stood back to let a pair of Great Danes sweep past majestically, and stopped for a moment to watch a class of magnificent Afghans being judged. Linda counted them in awe. "Thirty-two of them in just one class," she said. "And I thought twenty-three Kees were a lot!"

They found Katie and Paul at the far end of the handlers' tent, working on the snowy white coat of a Kuvasz. Gabriel was sound asleep in his crate. Katie, flushed with pleasure, accepted Mrs. Wentworth's congratulations on her handling, and gave Mrs. Wentworth the handful of ribbons Gabriel had won that morning.

Linda was on her knees beside the crate speaking lovingly to Gabriel. "Can I take him out for a minute?" she asked.

"No more than a minute," said Paul. "Wait, let me get the lead on him first."

"I know how to do that," Linda said, annoyed.

"Things are different at a show," Paul said firmly. "The dogs are on edge with excitement; everything is strange; even the old-timers feel the tension, and the young dogs most of all. You and Mrs. Wentworth may be here, but Katie and I are Gabriel's handlers and *we* are completely responsible for his safety, just as we are for each dog we have here today. What do you think would happen if Gabriel got loose right now?"

"Why, he'd be terrified," said Linda. "With all these strange dogs, and the noise, and the confusion. . . ."

"Exactly," said Paul. He opened the door of Gabriel's crate carefully, with his arm across the opening,

87

and let the door swing wide only when the lead was firmly snapped to the dog's collar.

"Hang onto that lead, whatever you do," cautioned Paul as he gave it to Linda. "Just last weekend a Shetland Sheepdog got away from its handler at a show and they still haven't found it."

Linda shuddered. Gabriel seemed quietly pleased to see her, and wagged his tail politely at Mrs. Wentworth. But, after the first greetings were over, he turned his head and looked longingly at his crate.

"He's tired," said Katie. "He really ought to rest, Linda."

"I would have thought a dog would hate being in a crate," said Linda, giving Gabriel a quick hug and handing his lead back to Paul. "But he actually seems to want to go in it."

"It's his retreat and his refuge," said Katie. "He can relax in a crate and know he's protected and safe."

Katie gave the Kuvasz a last sweep with the brush and lifted him off the grooming table. "Your turn, my lad," she said. The white dog yawned and stretched.

"*He* certainly doesn't seem tense," laughed Linda.

"He's been in this game a long time," said Paul. "This is old stuff to him. Wake up, Jupiter. If you go Best of Breed today, it will be your sixth in a row."

5 months

11

The weather changed abruptly during the night. Linda crawled out of bed the next morning and shuddered as she looked out of the window. The sky was dark and heavy with threatened rain, and a raw wind blew in short, strong gusts that whipped the branches of the trees beside the field.

"I can't believe they can hold a dog show on a day like this," she said to her mother, but a quick telephone call to the kennels told her that Katie and Paul had already left with the dogs.

Mrs. Wentworth had called the night before to tell Linda sadly that she had been sent to bed by her doctor. "Too much excitement for an old lady," she had explained in a tired voice. "No dog show for me tomorrow, I'm afraid."

"I'll take you to the show tomorrow," Mrs. Fairfax had told Linda. "I could use a day away from the typewriter, and I'd love to see Gabriel in a show. We'll pack a picnic and have lunch at the show; it will be lovely to get out in the sunshine and fresh air for a day."

But a fine, misty rain started as they turned into the show grounds. By the time they had found a parking place it had started to rain in earnest. Linda and her mother struggled across the open field toward the open-sided tents, clutching their raincoats around them, giggling as they splashed their way through the puddles already forming in the grass.

They plunged under the shelter of the nearest tent. Canvas billowed and snapped above them in the rising wind. The dog crates were pulled close together in the center of the tent, and towels and canvas coverings protected the dogs as much as possible from the cold, wet wind. As Linda and her mother stood, blinking the rain from their eyes and trying to find the ring numbers out in the rain-swept field, they saw Katie go by with a drenched Newfoundland. Neither Katie nor the dog seemed the least concerned.

Owners and handlers were ducking in and out of the tent, carrying their dogs if they were small enough, to keep them as dry and clean as possible under the circumstances. But it was impossible to carry the bigger breeds, and all the huge Newfoundlands, their classes finished, were hurrying back to the comparative shelter of the tent. Assistants waited with armloads of bath towels for the dogs and cups of steaming coffee for their handlers.

"I don't really believe any of this," said Mrs. Fairfax. She tugged her rain hat more firmly on her head and grinned at Linda. "You said the Kees were scheduled at 10:30, in ring 3. We'd better get out there if we want to see the judging."

Linda and her mother plunged out into the rain again, found the ring, and stood back away from it in shivering, excited silence. "Which one is Gabriel?" whispered Mrs. Fairfax as the dim gray shapes of the Kees formed in a line under the dark edge of the tent nearest their ring.

"Gosh, I don't know," Linda said. "It's too dark to tell one from another so far away! All I know is that Katie is wearing a blue raincoat and a white hat. That ought to help."

Five Kees moved out into the open ring with their handlers, and within a minute their heavy coats were soaked through. "That's Gabriel at the end of the line," whispered Linda. "Gosh, don't the Kees look funny when they're wet?"

The wind rose suddenly and the edges of the tent snapped like whips. Gabriel, safely at the farthest edge of the ring, merely turned his head and flattened his ears back for a moment, but one of the dogs, standing almost under the tent, whirled, yanked the lead out of his startled handler's hand, and bolted from the ring. There was one quick warning cry of "Loose dog!" and a spectator made a flying leap. It was over in a moment. Dripping muddy water, the man rose to his feet, triumphantly holding the terrified dog in his arms.

The grateful handler took the dog and returned to the ring. Patiently and with obvious care to move gently around the nervous dogs, the judge went on with the class. Few of the dogs would put their ears up for more than a few seconds at a time in the cold rain, but Gabriel didn't seem to mind. He stood like a rock with his sodden tail waving and his black ears pricked, his dark, shining eyes laughing up at Katie.

"He's having a wonderful time," whispered Linda fondly. "He thinks this whole thing is funny. Doesn't he look great? He'll certainly win easily today."

The judge finished going over the dogs, and motioned Katie to gait Gabriel. She started across the ring and Gabriel exploded into a capering whirlwind. Katie stopped, and the dog looked up at her with one foot raised, then started dancing with excitement. The wind blew a gust of rain across the ring right into his face. Gabriel sneezed, shook himself vigorously, and started to dance again on the end of his lead.

Linda held her breath. She could tell Katie was speaking to the dog; once she gave a sharp jerk of the lead. Gabriel's ears went back, his tail drooped for a moment, and he looked sadly up at Katie. She bent over and gave the dog a reassuring pat. Gabriel barked, just once, curled his wet tail over his back, and bounced along beside Katie like a rubber ball as she went on across the ring.

The judge shook her head and asked Katie to try to gait the dog again. But Gabriel would not trot for more than a few steps at a time.

"He's acting worse than those puppies did yesterday!" wailed Linda as she watched the dog prancing and capering across the ring. "Why doesn't Katie make him behave?"

All the other dogs gaited soberly beside their handlers, and Gabriel left the ring a few minutes later with the third-place yellow ribbon in Katie's wet hand.

"We can go and see him now," Linda said in a disgusted voice. "He's through for today. Dumb dog."

She and her mother ducked their heads against the rain, which seemed, in their disappointment, to have become colder and wetter than it had been before.

They found Katie and Paul rubbing Gabriel with enormous towels.

"Oh, Katie, wasn't he *awful?*" Linda was close to tears.

"He was young," said Katie cheerfully, reaching for a fresh towel. Gabriel, who was lying on the grooming table enjoying all the attention, wagged his tail at Linda and took the edge of the towel in his teeth and shook it.

"Just look at him!" said Linda. "He's acting like a silly puppy!"

"Exactly." Katie made growling noises back at Gabriel, taking a moment to play with the delighted dog. "There, just settle down now." She gave him a quick pat and went back to rubbing him dry.

"I don't understand," said Linda. "Couldn't you *make* him behave?"

"Showing a young dog is tricky," Katie explained patiently. "Certainly he acted like an idiot out there today, but he was a happy idiot, in spite of the wind and the rain and the flapping tent and the flapping raincoats and the other disturbing things all happening at once."

"It's a mistake to expect too much too soon from a young dog," said Paul. "If you lean on a young one too hard—if you put too much pressure on him in the ring before he's old enough and experienced enough to take it—he'll start to think of showing as an unpleasant chore. O.K., we lost possible points today because Katie didn't force Gabriel to behave. But what do you think will happen the next time he's shown under tough conditions? He'll remember that this was a happy experience and that Katie didn't scold him for having a good time in the ring.

"The next time she can remind him to behave himself a little better. Gradually, as he gets more experience, he'll settle down."

"But won't Mrs. Wentworth be disappointed?" asked Linda.

"She's shown dogs for a good many years," said Paul. "We'll call her this evening to tell her about the show, and she'll be as pleased as we are that Gabriel wasn't frightened or bothered by all of this." He waved his hand toward the storm outside the tent. He scooped Gabriel up in his arms and put him in a crate deeply piled with dry towels. "There," he said, latching the door securely, "he'll be warm enough now. Katie, I've got the Boxer to go in ten minutes."

"And I've got the Bernese Mountain Dog just after

that," said Katie. "Thank goodness weather doesn't bother this one." She brought the huge dog out of his crate. He blinked calmly at the sheets of rain blowing outside the tent.

"He's an experienced campaigner," Katie said, rubbing the big dog's head with affection. "No surprises any more for you, are there?" She ran a brush over the shining coat, struggled back into her wet raincoat, and disappeared into the rain.

"Crazy!" muttered Linda as she and her mother drove home with the heater on full and the windshield wipers beating frantically at the pouring rain.

"I had no idea, absolutely no idea, that showing a dog could be so complicated." Mrs. Fairfax slowed up as the car moved through a flooded dip in the road. "Or so cold or wet. Aren't there any *indoor* dog shows?"

"This is the last outdoor show around here this year," said Linda. "They'll all be inside from now on, until next spring." Linda brushed back her wet hair and giggled. "But, after today, I shouldn't think *anything* would bother Gabriel, indoors or out!"

1 year

12 Linda leaned on the lower half of the grooming-room door, listening with breathless pleasure as a V of Canada geese swept overhead. They were flying low enough so that she could hear their call and even the soft murmuring rustle of their wings.

"Wonderful," she whispered. "Just wonderful."

She hadn't heard Paul stop behind her and she was startled when he spoke to her. "You really like it here, don't you, Linda?"

Linda flushed and turned. "We're staying another six months, at least," she said. "Mother made the arrangements yesterday. She needs more time for her book. And I've already started school—" She leaned dreamily on the door again, looking out over the fields and woods surrounding the kennels. "Anyway, I don't think either of us wants to leave, to tell the absolute truth."

There was a comfortable silence. The dogs in the kennels were quiet. The only sound was the fading cry of the geese and a soft, low whimpering from Mandy, the old Golden Retriever, who had come out into her run and was standing facing the disappearing geese.

Paul spoke in a low voice to the old dog, who swung toward him with a sharp bark of joy. Her tail wagged frantically as she sat and lifted one paw pleadingly toward Paul. "No more, old lady, no more," said Paul. He cleared his throat. "We had some good times together, didn't we, old girl? But it's your puppies that are grown and out there now. The water's too cold and the geese are too heavy for you, Mandy. . . ." Paul took a deep breath. "Got to get Tiger here into a tub," he said gruffly, rumpling the ears of the small white terrier he was carrying under his arm. "His owners are coming for him tonight."

Mandy turned sadly away and curled up in the run, facing the direction the geese had gone. "What can I do?" said Linda restlessly. "All my chores are finished. It's such a beautiful afternoon, and it's too early to put the dogs away. Could I take Gabriel outside for a walk? Both of us are tired of staying in that same old fenced field in the back."

Paul hesitated for a moment, then finally nodded. "Be sure to keep him on a lead and out of the woods," he cautioned. "He's going to the Boston show in three weeks and we don't want his coat torn up with burrs."

"Great!" Linda dashed into the office to snatch a lead from the rack. "Just don't let him run off," called Paul toward Linda's retreating back. Linda waved to show she had heard. All these warnings annoyed her. After all, hadn't she raised the dog from a tiny puppy —and done a good job, too, or he wouldn't be as beautiful as he was now. . . .

In a few minutes, her brief annoyance gone, she was running down a wide path, with Gabriel bounding joyously beside her.

There had been a hard frost, but Indian summer now lay warm and golden over the countryside. Corn shocks stood evenly in the stubbled fields and an occasional forgotten pumpkin glowed like an orange flame against the gray stone walls. Linda slowed to a walk.

They went through an open gate into a field and Gabriel stopped to investigate the possibility of field mice hiding in a dried shock of corn. Holding the lead tightly, Linda let him paw at the rustling corn, and laughed as he poked his short black muzzle between the bound stalks, his tightly curled silver tail quivering with excitement.

Gabriel barked. A half-grown rabbit scurried out of the corn and bounced rapidly away across the field. Gabriel lunged after the rabbit but was stopped at the end of the lead. Then, in one fleeting second, he whipped around to face Linda, ducked his head, and slipped the light show lead over his ears. In silent, joyous determination, he flew like a furry bullet after the running rabbit. In a few moments the field was empty. Both rabbit and Gabriel had disappeared.

"No," whispered Linda, staring blankly at the limp lead in her hand.

She started to run, shouting Gabriel's name. She stumbled over the rough corn stubble, and finally reached the end of the field, looking wildly into the heavy woods on the other side of the stone wall. She struggled for breath, trying to listen for the sound of barking. She called Gabriel again, but her only answer was the mocking echo of a flock of crows deep in the woods.

"*Gabriel!*" She gave one last, despairing call. For an instant, the crows were silent, and Linda heard the stabbing cry of a dog in pain.

Heedless of the briers that tore at her arms and legs,

100

Linda jumped down from the wall and ran into the woods. Her heart was pounding so hard she was afraid she could not hear, but faintly, close by, she could make out the whimpers of the dog. She found a narrow, winding pathway and followed it as well as she could until she stumbled around a huge old oak and found Gabriel.

The dog was lying in a pile of fallen leaves. He was silent now, with his muzzle on the ground, looking up at Linda with a terrified expression in his dark eyes. Her whole body shaking with sobs of relief, Linda flung herself to her knees beside him. But Gabriel didn't move or raise his head.

With enormous effort, Linda stopped her crying and stared through tear-blurred eyes at the motionless dog. She put out a shaking hand and touched his head. He whimpered once, but didn't move. With growing fear, Linda very gently began to move the leaves away, and in a moment her hand felt the icy steel of the trap which had snapped shut on the dog's front leg.

The woods spun and tipped around her. Linda rocked back on her heels and put her hands over her face. She had never fainted in her life, but she wondered, dimly, if she wasn't about to do so now. There was a funny humming in her ears and when she tried to open her eyes, everything looked dim and gray and

101

far away. She shut her eyes again quickly, and pushed her hair away from her sweating face.

Gradually, the grayness passed, the humming in her ears faded, and everything came back into focus. With grim determination, keeping her eyes carefully away from the dog's pleading look, she examined the rusty trap.

It was fastened by a thin, strong chain to the base of the oak tree. No hope of breaking the chain or of tearing it away from the tree. And Linda had no idea how to open a trap. She had never seen one before.

It was obvious it had a very strong spring. Gritting her teeth, she put her hands on the curved bars holding Gabriel's leg, then stopped. Suppose she got the trap half open, but couldn't hold it, and it snapped shut again on the dog? Linda jerked her hands back as though she had been burned.

"Gabriel, I've got to go get help." The suffering dog looked up at her in silence. "Gabriel, it's awful to leave you here. But you must understand, you *must*, I can't help you alone. I'm going to get Paul, Gabriel." She rested her hand lightly on the dog's head and then rose determinedly to her feet.

The dog made no sound. Linda pushed her way firmly down the faint track of the rabbit path that led back toward the corn field. Though she knew she was making a terrible mistake, she couldn't stop herself from turning to take one more look at the trapped dog. He had raised his head at last and was looking at her in silence, his eyes so full of pain and despair that Linda thought, for one ghastly moment, that she was going to be sick.

She whirled back to the path, trying to shut the memory of the dog's pleading eyes from her mind, trying to keep from running because she knew she could not run all the way back to the kennels and would make better time if she kept to a fast walk—

She burst into the kennels, hoping wildly that her shaking knees would hold her up just a little bit longer. Katie and Paul were both in the office. They rose to their feet in shocked surprise at the sight of Linda's tear-streaked face.

"It's Gabriel," Linda said flatly. "He's caught in a trap, and I don't know how to get him out."

Paul snatched the car keys from the hook on the wall. "Where?" he asked.

"In the woods beyond the corn field," answered Linda.

Katie reached for the phone. "I'll have the vet meet you at his office," she said.

Linda could hear the whirl of the dial as she ran after Paul, who was already in the Jeep with the engine running. He waited only for Linda to fling herself onto the seat beside him before throwing the sturdy engine into gear and roaring down the bumpy path that led to the field. Linda pointed in silence to the wall nearest Gabriel. Without a word, Paul jerked to a stop. Linda was out and ahead of him in a moment, scrambling over the wall to lead the way.

As they pushed their way through the thick woods, Linda wondered in a brief flash of panic if it could be possible for them not to find the trapped dog. Her teeth clamped down on her lower lip hard enough to hurt. This kind of wild thinking was stupid and no help at all to Gabriel. There was the huge oak—she knew where she was now—and then Paul was kneeling beside the still form of the dog, murmuring to him in cheerful reassuring sounds as his strong hands forced the jaws of the trap apart. Linda gently pulled Gabriel's leg free.

Without a wasted moment, Paul lifted the limp dog in his arms and led the way back to the waiting Jeep. "In the back, Linda," he said. "Hold the dog." With one arm holding the dog on the seat and the other holding his head on her lap, Linda braced her feet against the floor to keep her balance as the car bucked and swayed over the field and out onto the nearest road.

1 year

13 Linda sat in the waiting room staring numbly at the gray wall. The door to the examining room was open and, when she turned her head, she could see the tip of Gabriel's tail and the backs of Paul and the veterinarian as they worked over the dog.

"He's in shock," she heard the doctor say. "Stay beside him, Paul—rub him behind the ears—there—he didn't even feel the needle. Good. He ought to pick up in a minute."

The men's voices dropped to a low murmur. Linda thought vaguely that she had time to cry now, but couldn't.

106

"O.K., bring him along, Paul. We'll get an x-ray of that leg and see what the damage is." They carried Gabriel off to another room.

In her mind, Linda could picture the x-rays of Gabriel's leg. It was almost as though she could hear Katie saying, "Heidi was a lovely dog, but her leg was so badly broken she never could go back to the show ring—"

Linda squeezed her eyes shut and leaned her head back against the wall. Suppose Gabriel's leg was so badly broken that nothing could be done? Did they ever shoot dogs with broken legs, the way she heard they so often did with horses? Linda opened her eyes and stood up abruptly. Waiting and wondering—afraid to hope for the best—were almost unbearable.

With a guilty start, Linda realized that it was getting dark and her mother didn't know where she was. She switched on the light and used the phone on the receptionist's desk, telling her mother what had happened in short, quick sentences. Mrs. Fairfax was concerned, but asked no unnecessary questions. Linda hung up gratefully and went back to staring at the wall.

It was almost an hour before the doctor came out to the waiting room and put his hand on Linda's shoulder.

"The x-rays show no damage to the bone," he said. "I've x-rayed that leg from every possible angle, just to make sure, and we'll x-ray again in three or four weeks, but there's very little doubt that this dog's leg will be as good as new. Of course, there's been a lot of bruising and there will be a lot of swelling. He's not going to be able to walk on that leg for some time. But he's going to be all right."

Paul came to join them, grinning with relief.

"Where is Gabriel?" whispered Linda.

"Stop worrying," the doctor said comfortably. "I'm going to keep him here for a day or two, and then you can have him back."

Linda huddled miserably in the front seat of the car. Paul whistled softly as he drove down the darkening roads.

"I don't see how you can be so calm," Linda burst out suddenly, turning to face Paul at last. "You *told* me to be careful. Now Gabriel's hurt, and it was all my fault. Aren't you even angry?"

"Linda," said Paul gravely, "believe it or not, Katie are I are human, too. Both of us have worked with animals for a long, long time. We've done our share of dumb things, too. Accidents are always stupid. Some of them are heartbreaking. But you try to avoid them.

108

Most important, if they happen, you try to learn something from them."

He braked and turned into the lane leading up to Linda's house. "You were responsible for Gabriel this afternoon. You were careless, and he got hurt. But we were all lucky—Katie and I because we still have one of the most promising youngsters we've had to handle in several years, Mrs. Wentworth because she still has her irreplaceable Harborlight dog . . . and you were lucky." He stopped at the front door of the house and smiled at Linda. "So was Gabriel."

Paul and Katie left in a whirling snowstorm to drive to the Boston show. Gabriel watched the preparations with excitement, hobbling about in his pen on three legs. When the camper full of dogs and crates left without him, he was upset and bewildered. For the first two days he would not eat and either sat watching the door and listening for the return of the camper, or curled up in a shaggy silver ball in the corner of his pen.

Linda was frantic, but Mr. and Mrs. Wilder, who were there caring for the dogs as they always did when Katie and Paul were away, were sympathetic but unworried.

"We've seen this many times before," they assured Linda. "There are some dogs that grieve and some that don't. The grievers are the real show dogs, for sure. They love it and miss it and can't bear to be left out of it."

Linda hoped they were right and that there was nothing else wrong with Gabriel. She was enormously relieved when Katie and Paul came back, and expected to find Gabriel his old, happy self when she rushed into the kennels from school that afternoon.

Instead, to her horror, she found the dog sitting with his back to the aisle, paying no attention as Katie moved through the kennels.

"*Now* what's the matter with him?" Linda asked despairingly. "He's sick, I just know he's sick. Shouldn't you take his temperature? Shouldn't you call the vet?"

Much to Linda's astonishment, Katie laughed. "Watch this," said Katie. She stopped by Gabriel's pen and spoke to the dog cheerfully. Gabriel glanced at her. Linda saw the very tip of his tail wag, just once, then the dog turned his head deliberately away from Katie and looked firmly at the blank wall.

"That is truly what is called getting the cold shoulder," said Katie. "He's jealous and upset and mad at me for leaving him behind. Some of the show dogs react this way. He's certainly one of them! By tomorrow he'll forgive me. Just wait and see."

Katie was right. By the next afternoon, Gabriel was up and happy, wolfing down his food and prancing in his pen as well as he could with one paw still held in the air.

"I sure wish that leg of his would get better so he could go to another show with you," said Linda. "When is he going to start walking on it again?"

"Should be pretty soon," said Paul.

But the weeks went by, the swelling disappeared, and still Gabriel would do no more than hobble on his leg, barely putting his paw on the ground. More x-rays were taken. Nothing could be found which would cause Gabriel's continuing lameness.

One Saturday morning Linda arrived at the kennels to find Gabriel looking mournful and sorry for himself, holding one paw up pathetically. It was heavily bandaged.

"Oh, you poor thing," wailed Linda, unlatching the gate and kneeling down to hug the dog. "What happened?" Gabriel sighed and buried his head against Linda's comforting arms.

"Poor Gabriel." Paul leaned over the pen and looked at the dog sympathetically. Then, to Linda's astonishment, he grinned and winked at her. Puzzled, Linda gave Gabriel a last loving pat, shut the gate carefully, and followed Paul to the office.

"What's so funny?" she demanded heatedly.

Katie, rummaging in the closet for a new clipping blade, smiled over her shoulder at Linda. "Didn't you notice?" she said. "Probably not, because he's putting on quite an act of being very sorry for himself. The bandage is on the right paw, Linda. It was the left leg that was in the trap."

"And it's working beautifully," said Paul with satisfaction. "In two days we'll take the bandage off, and he won't be able to remember which paw he's supposed to limp on. Neither of them hurt, Linda. But he liked the fuss and attention his injured leg was getting. Dr. Peterson is a very good vet, and, in his opinion, Gabriel's leg is as sound now as it ever was. If he's right, and I'll bet he is, when we take that bandage off his other paw in two days, Gabriel will be perfectly all right again."

Two days later, with great ceremony, the fake bandage was removed from Gabriel's paw. Katie lifted the dog from the grooming table and put him gently on the floor. Katie, Paul, and Linda stood silently watching the dog.

Gabriel sat down, looking puzzled, and shifted his weight from one front paw to the other. He got up, took a few uncertain steps, then swung around to Linda with his dark eyes sparkling and his tail wagging.

"Great," said Linda, blinking back tears of relief as Gabriel trotted happily across the grooming-room floor.

"We're back in business again," said Katie.

"I'm going to call Dr. Peterson to tell him he was right again," said Paul. "And then I'm going to call Mrs. Wentworth. Katie, it's a darned good thing you went ahead and entered that dog at the Garden."

1 year

14 The traffic snarled and howled through the city streets. Linda made a face as she stumbled out of the taxi and stood, shivering in the raw February wind, waiting for her mother to pay the fare, and squinting up at the huge sign over her head. Madison Square Garden. Westminster Dog Show.

It was strange to think that Gabriel was here, in the middle of New York—Gabriel and about three thousand other dogs, Linda reminded herself. It seemed stranger still to walk into the warmth of the Garden where she had come with her mother when they had lived in New York, always as a spectator, always.

114

seated high above the Garden floor, disconnected from anything that was happening below.

But today was different. The wide doors were open into the arena and the huge Garden echoed eerily with the sound of barking dogs. The floor was divided into the familiar pattern of dog-show rings. Owners and handlers, dogs and judges, ring stewards and photographers, the announcer's voice on the loudspeaker, calling for different breeds to get ready for judging—everything was the same as it always was at any show, and yet—Linda shivered again, this time with excitement.

Everything was not the same as it always was at other shows, because they were *other* shows. Only *this* was the Garden.

The soft lighting glowed on the dogs as they gaited and posed in the rings with their handlers. Linda and her mother made their way slowly down the crowded center aisle, stopping to admire a particularly beautiful Irish Setter, dodging out of the way of a tense-faced handler who hurried by with two Old English Sheepdogs beside him.

"He's going to get those poor dogs all upset," said Linda with professional disapproval. "Dogs don't like to be rushed about like that." She stopped, and her voice rose with excitement. "Look, over there!

115

There're Paul and Katie with two of the Newfound-lands."

They edged their way over to the side of the ring. The two big white and black dogs gaited with cheerful dignity. All the other Newfoundlands in the ring were black.

"I didn't even know they came in black and white," said Mrs. Fairfax.

"There're not very many that color," said Linda, "and it's harder to win with them. They're called Landseers."

"You're learning a great deal about these things," said her mother with interest.

Linda nodded her head. "I've got to," she said. "I'm going to be a vet one day."

Her mother raised her eyebrows, then smiled. "Why not?" she said thoughtfully. "Why not, indeed?"

They watched the rest of the class, applauding enthusiastically when Paul won with the dog he was handling and Katie was second with hers.

They made their way through the wide doors at the end of the arena into the back section of the Garden, where long rows of high wooden benches, partitioned into stalls, held more than fifteen hundred dogs.

"I never saw so many dogs in my life," gasped Mrs. Fairfax.

116

"This is only half of them," said Linda. "The rest come to be shown tomorrow. There's not enough room at the Garden for all the breeds to be here on the same day.

"Katie said the handlers' section would be on the right, toward the back. Let's see if we can find her."

They struggled through the crowded aisles. Some of the dogs were barking and a few were howling, but most of them sat quietly in their comfortable wire bench crates, soberly watching the people and the other dogs, or sleeping peacefully.

"The dogs have to be on their assigned benches until one hour before they're due to be judged," explained Linda, "so Gabriel won't be back in the handlers' section yet. Kees are judged at 1:30, and it's only 11:15 now."

In spite of the confusion, they soon found the tables and crates where the handlers were preparing their dogs for the ring. It was quieter here. The handlers spoke in low voices as they brushed and trimmed their charges, and the sweet smell of chalk and talcum powder and coat dressing hung in the air.

They saw Katie and Paul leading the gentle Newfoundlands to their grooming section where two assistants, who helped them at the bigger shows, waited to take them in charge.

117

"They both need a drink of fresh water, and then give them a chance to exercise before you put them back on the benches," Katie was saying, patting each dog and handing their leads to the assistants. "And don't worry about the Boxer. Mr. Kent has just gone to get him." She turned to face Linda and her mother with a smile. "Hi, I thought I saw you earlier. What do you think of all this?"

"Incredible," said Mrs. Fairfax.

"How is Gabriel?" asked Linda.

"He's O.K.," answered Katie, turning to busy herself rolling leads and tucking them away neatly into the tack crate drawer.

Linda knew Katie well enough by now to understand what she meant. "O.K." meant reasonably happy. Probably the bustling crowds and the strangeness of his first indoor benched show were upsetting the young dog, at least a little. It was bound to happen, since his hurt leg had prevented him from going to the other indoor shows in which he'd been entered for experience. Linda felt an enormous wave of guilt.

"Try not to worry too much," said Katie with understanding. "Even though Gabriel's only been shown twice before this, they were good experiences and he sailed through them with real confidence in himself. Once he finds out all this fuss in the Garden means

118

just another dog show, he'll probably bounce out of that benching crate as though he's been here for years."

Linda felt better, but then Paul came up with the handsome fawn Boxer dancing beside him and her heart sank again as she heard Katie ask anxiously, "How was Gabriel when you checked him last, Paul?"

"He's coming along fine," said Paul. "He even drank a little water. He's lying down now and he's beginning to look relaxed. He's watching all the goings on but he doesn't seem worried. Just interested."

"Great," said Katie with a quick smile toward Linda. The Boxer flung himself joyfully at Katie. "O.K., bonehead, settle down," she said fondly. She patted the dog, lifted him up on the grooming table, and reached for a soft cloth. Linda and her mother moved away; Katie and Paul had work to do. There would be time for talking later.

Linda's mother suggested lunch at noon. Linda gazed at her in horror. Excitement was building inside her almost unbearably; the very thought of food made her feel sick. "Maybe later," she mumbled, and her mother, understanding, agreed.

And then, at last, it was 1:30. Ring 4 was cleared and the new judge came in. He checked his watch, made a note in his book, then nodded to the steward, who motioned the first Keeshond to come into the ring.

Linda had planned to analyze each dog with care. She was going to mark her catalogue with brief words and notes of comparison, but the catalogue grew limp in her hand and the pencil dropped, unnoticed, to the floor. The ring seemed to whirl and grow blurry with a ruffled pattern of silver and gray, waving tails and dancing dark eyes. Swift moment of panic. *Where was Gabriel?*

Linda blinked and held her breath, then let it out with a sigh of relief. He was there with Katie, just outside the ring. Katie slipped the yellow armband with Gabriel's number on it over her sleeve, patted the dog quietly, and led him through the gate.

Katie walked briskly across the ring and Gabriel trotted along beside her, then suddenly stopped and froze in his tracks. Katie stopped too, and patted the dog again. He moved forward with a peculiar, mincing gait and Linda suddenly realized what was the matter —Gabriel had never before felt the texture of the green matting which covered the ring to keep the dogs from slipping on the polished Garden floor. It was clear that he was puzzled either by the way the matting felt under his feet or by the whispering sound it made

120

as he moved. He put his ears back and sniffed the matting suspiciously. Katie let him alone.

Gabriel looked up, shook himself vigorously, and wagged his tail at Katie. She gave him a scrap of liver and gaited him a few steps, then stopped and gave him another piece. The mats were forgotten, and Gabriel trotted cheerfully beside Katie as they took their place in line.

The class began. The dogs and their handlers moved in a wide circle around the ring. Each dog was judged individually, gaited individually, and then three dogs were chosen to come to the center of the ring. One was Gabriel.

"The darker, bigger dog, number 5, is from Texas," said Mrs. Fairfax, having taken the catalogue from Linda's numb hand and found the Keeshond classes. "The other one's from California."

Linda barely heard and could not answer. There was nothing in the world at that moment but the softly lit ring, the three posing Kees, the judge, and the feeling of time standing still.

The judge moved from one dog to the next. Katie, looking cool and unruffled in her smooth blue dress, lightly tossed a scrap of dried liver in one hand as Gabriel watched eagerly. He was standing like a black

121

and silver statue on the end of the slack lead, with his ears pricked high and his tail wagging gently.

A wooden folding chair fell over at the ringside with a rattling crash. Most of the dogs were startled; one of the three dogs in the center of the ring spun away from his handler in sudden fright. Though the handler held the lead firmly, the damage was done; the plumed tail uncurled and the dog, with a worried look, kept his ears flat back against his head.

"That's a shame," murmured Linda, and felt a fleeting stab of guilt because she knew very well she wasn't a bit sorry; this kind of thing, as Katie and Paul had often said, was just part of the game, and this time the luck had been with Gabriel. He was unconcerned and had barely glanced at the fallen chair.

The frightened Keeshond would not gait properly. Gabriel and the other dog were asked to gait side by side. Again, time came to a stop. The judge stood, his hands clasped behind him, looking down at the two beautiful dogs.

The judge straightened up. He lifted his hand, and waved Katie and Gabriel to the first-place marker at the side of the ring.

Linda burst into tears. She felt like an idiot until she saw her mother was blinking as well.

"I am a wreck," said Mrs. Fairfax in a shaking voice,

122

"a complete and utter wreck. I think I would have screamed if that class had lasted one more minute. Come on, Linda, let's go congratulate Katie and Gabriel!"

"You can't," sniffed Linda, groping for a handkerchief in her pocket. "We can't let Gabriel know we're here. That's only the Open class he's won. He's got to go back in the ring again soon to compete for Winners Dog."

"Very well," said Mrs. Fairfax with a sigh. "I hope I can stand it."

The Winners class did not last very long. The judge was familiar with each of the dogs, having seen them in their previous classes. In a few minutes, with her face flushed with pleasure, Katie led Gabriel from the ring with the purple Winners rosette fluttering from her hand.

Linda, her hair falling over her eyes, was searching frantically on the floor for her pencil. "I meant to mark my catalogue," she wailed, "and now I can't remember anything but Gabriel!"

"Linda, what on earth is happening now?" asked Mrs. Fairfax. "Katie's back in the ring with him again!"

"Glory, I forgot," gasped Linda, jumping to her feet. "The Winners Dog and Winners Bitch both compete now with the champions for Best of Breed."

The ring was filled again with Kees. "All of them are champions in there now, except for Gabriel, of course, and the one that went Winners Bitch."

"Mmmn . . . that would be number 18," said Mrs. Fairfax.

"She's awfully pretty," said Linda. She felt much calmer now, and limp with relief. Gabriel's part was really over. This class for Best of Breed was only a formality for the young dog. All the other Kees in the ring now were Champions of Record, and they were older, more mature, and far more experienced. Some of them had been to the Garden two or three years in succession. They represented the finest Keeshond bloodlines from all parts of the world.

"Gabriel's lit up like a Christmas tree." Linda giggled. "You'd think he'd be tired by now, but he's having a wonderful time! I guess he's just a show-off at heart."

Gabriel bounced beside Katie as they waited for the class to begin. The judge moved to the center of the ring. Katie spoke to Gabriel; Linda could see her lips moving and, this time, the dog obediently settled down to a more sedate trot as the handlers gaited their dogs.

Linda half-watched the judging of the class. Gabriel

had done wonderfully well, it had been a marvelous day—he now had nine points toward the fifteen he needed for his championship—

She stopped counting points in her head and stared in shocked silence at the ring. There had been a burst of applause, the judge was moving back to the table, and it was Gabriel who was standing alone with Katie in the center of the ring.

"He didn't. He couldn't," said Linda.

"But he did," said her mother. "Gabriel's won Best of Breed at the Garden."

A few minutes later, the Keeshond judging was over. Two or three other handlers stopped to shake hands with Katie before leaving the ring with their dogs. Then photographs were taken of the judge and Katie and Gabriel, who was enchanted by the photographer's flashing lights.

The judge thanked his stewards and left. Katie stopped to give Gabriel a quick hug, then led him out of the ring. A cluster of black and white Dalmatians with their handlers spilled through the gate and fanned out across the ring floor.

"I guess this time it's really over," said Linda in a dazed voice. "No more surprises today. It's all so wonderful I can't even think straight. Now let's go find Gabriel."

1 year

15 Katie was sitting on a grooming table, looking limp and tired. Jim, one of her assistants, was bringing her a cup of coffee as Linda and her mother made their way through the handlers' section.

"Showing a dog looks so easy from outside the ring," murmured Linda's mother thoughtfully. "But I'm beginning to realize what incredible pressure there must be. . . ."

Katie's face brightened as she caught sight of them.

"I don't know what to say," said Linda. "I just can't think of any words."

"Gabriel is a very special dog," said Katie, "and this has been his very special day. With a little bit of luck,

127

it should be the first of many."

A dark-haired man with a thin smile and quick, narrow eyes slipped between two grooming tables and reached out to shake Katie's hand. "Congratulations," he said. "It isn't easy to go all the way to Best of Breed like that with a young dog up from the Open class. Haven't seen you out with a Kees for some time. Not so easy to get hold of a good one, eh? I thought old lady Wentworth was dead years ago, and then there you were, hiding in the corner of the ring with another one of her darned Harborlight dogs. Looks a lot like old Mariner, doesn't he?"

Katie retrieved her hand as quickly as possible. "Thank you," she said in a stiff, formal voice. "He's a nice young dog and shows a lot of promise."

Linda scowled at the man's back. The tone of his voice and Katie's response made her uncomfortable.

"Better be on my way. Hoped to see your youngster up close, but I guess Paul's got him in the exercise pen? I'll have a look at him there. Got a couple of Shepherds to exercise, anyway."

He vanished into the crowd with an airy wave of his hand. "Watch him, Jim," said Katie quickly to the assistant standing beside her. "Tell Paul." Jim asked no questions. In an instant he was gone.

Linda was wild with curiosity. "What's happening?" she said. "What's the matter? Who was that man?"

Katie sighed. "He's a handler who's been around a long time, and he's the kind the profession can do without! He's been suspended twice, and if he gets into any more trouble, the Kennel Club will take his handler's license away from him permanently. But he's got a sneaky way of doing things and he's hard to catch.

"Gabriel's a threat, now. He's made the big leagues. He's beaten a lot of good dogs, he's on his way up, and not everyone is as happy about it as we are, you can be sure!"

There was a long silence. Linda and her mother glanced at each other uneasily. Suddenly, from the nearby exercise pen, there was an uproar of snarling and barking. Somebody shouted. Katie whipped off the grooming table but, before she could take more than a step, Paul was there to put out a reassuring hand.

"Everything's all right," he said. "Jim told me, and Fred did just what you thought he would. Brought that bad-tempered Shepherd into the exercise pen and just happened to turn him loose next to Gabriel. You remember that dog, Katie. He's the one that attacked the Rottweiler, for no reason at all, last fall at the Ox Ridge show."

Linda jumped to her feet with a cry of alarm. "What about Gabriel? Is he hurt?"

Paul shook his head with great satisfaction. "Never

knew anything about it. Jim is sharp. He had his eye on the Shepherd and got Gabriel out of the pen so fast his head is probably still spinning! And there were witnesses. I don't think Fred will dare to bother us again."

Katie looked up at him questioningly. "Don't worry," said Paul. "Jim will stay where he can watch Gabriel while he's on the bench for the rest of the day. Just in case."

Linda sat down again quickly. Her knees were shaking. "What an awful thing to do," she whispered.

"What was Fred's particular problem today, Katie?" asked Paul. "Do you have any idea?"

Katie nodded and showed Paul the dog show catalogue. "I looked it up," she said. "He's been handling that good Bulldog of Mr. Roundtree's, the one they brought over from Europe last summer. I think Fred had his eye on the Non-Sporting Group tonight, and Gabriel's got him worried." She slapped the catalogue down on the crate. She managed to smile at Linda and her mother. "Great compliment to Gabriel, anyway."

"What is this 'group' I keep hearing about?" asked Mrs. Fairfax. "And what has it got to do with Gabriel?"

"All breeds of dogs recognized by the American Kennel Club are divided into six separate groups,"

130

said Paul. "There's the Sporting Group, which includes all the spaniels, retrievers, and pointers; the Hound Group, which includes breeds such as the Foxhound and the Beagle and the Greyhound; the Working Group, which includes the shepherd breeds such as the Collie, and the sled dogs and guard dogs. Then there's the Terrier Group, with the Fox Terriers, the Scottie, the Skye, and all the other terrier breeds. The Toy Group has the Toy Poodles, and Pomeranians, and several other small breeds. And then there's the Non-Sporting Group, which includes such breeds as the Chow, the bigger Poodles, the Bulldog—and the Keeshond."

"All Best of Breed winners in the show compete against each other in their own groups," Katie went on. "The Working, Terrier, and Non-Sporting Groups will be held tonight. Then, tomorrow, when all the rest of the breeds and groups have been judged, the six group winners will compete against each other for Best in Show."

"Oh, wow," Linda whispered. "You mean Gabriel's going to be out there tonight, with all those other fantastic dogs? Will his name be in the newspaper?"

"He'll be there." Katie smiled. "But you must remember, Linda, he's very young. Don't expect too much of him too soon."

131

"Still—" said Linda. "It's kind of fun to have him winning."

"Winning isn't everything," cautioned Mrs. Fairfax.

Linda laughed. "Linus said the same thing, once, in a *Peanuts* cartoon, and Charlie Brown's answer was, 'That's true, but losing isn't ANYTHING.' "

Everyone smiled. "Don't worry, we'll stay tonight," said Mrs. Fairfax. "Wild horses couldn't drag me out of this place until Gabriel's part is over, win or lose."

They saw Paul raise his hand in a gesture that was a wave, but looked more like a welcoming salute. Katie and Linda both rose to their feet; the tall, proud figure of Mrs. Wentworth was coming toward them.

"I looked, but I couldn't find her anywhere," whispered Linda. "I hope she saw Gabriel in the ring!"

"My dear." Mrs. Wentworth's smile was for all of them, but her hands reached out for Katie's. "You have made me very, very happy today, as you have so often in the past." She turned to Linda and put one hand out to touch her cheek. The hand was cool but there were two bright patches of color burning on Mrs. Wentworth's pale cheeks, and her eyes were bright with happiness. "It was lovely, perfectly lovely, to see a Harborlight dog at the Garden again."

Katie picked up a bright handful of rosettes from the tack crate drawer beside her. "You might like to see these," she said as she handed them to Linda. "We've all worked hard for them!"

Then she took a small box from the pocket of her skirt and held it out to Mrs. Wentworth with a quiet smile.

Mrs. Wentworth took the box and opened it gently. Inside was a silver medal which glowed in the soft Garden light. On the medal were the words *Westminster Kennel Club*, in raised letters, and the figure of a Pointer, the symbol of the Club.

"What a pretty thing!" Linda said admiringly. "Is it yours?"

"No, my dear, it belongs to Gabriel," Mrs. Wentworth said. "This is the medal he won for Best of Breed today. But, for the first time in my life, I am going to keep something that doesn't belong to me. I would like to have this mounted beside the one Mariner won here, so many years ago."

There was a moment of shared happy silence. Mrs. Wentworth snapped the box shut and tucked it safely in her purse, then drew out two long envelopes. She handed a dark yellow one to Katie. "You will understand when you read this," she said. "My lawyer's name is there in case you or Paul have any questions. But it should all be quite clear. The joy of your clients doesn't feed the dogs or pay for their handling and entry fees! If Gabriel lives up to his promise, he may be with you for many successful years. I want him to go on, Katie. I have established a fund for this, and shall ask you to bill the bank directly after today."

Katie nodded in understanding silence.

"And you, young lady." Mrs. Wentworth turned to Linda. "This is for you."

Linda took the long white envelope with a puzzled frown. It had already been opened. She drew out a rectangular paper, edged with a border of purple, and recognized the seal of the American Kennel Club. On the back she saw her own name, that day's date, and Mrs. Wentworth's signature.

"Oh!" whispered Katie, who had immediately recognized the paper for what it was.

Linda looked up at her. "It's Gabriel's registration certificate," said Katie. "Mrs. Wentworth has transferred him to your name. You own him now, Linda."

Linda swung toward Mrs. Wentworth, stunned into silence.

"Don't try to thank me, child," Mrs. Wentworth said softly. "It is I who should thank you for sharing Gabriel." She touched Linda's face again lightly. "Take good care of him. It is lovely to know the Harborlight name will go on with such honor."

Linda stared blankly at the certificate in her hand. Paul had vanished, and now was back with Gabriel. He put the delighted dog on the grooming table. Gabriel sat down and reached out with one paw.

Mrs. Wentworth took the paw gravely in her hand. "Good-by, young fellow. Your grandfather would have been proud of you."

"But you can't be *leaving*," gasped Linda, finding her voice at last. "He's going to be in the Group tonight—"

"I know." Mrs. Wentworth smiled sadly. "But months ago my doctors insisted I move to a warmer climate. Everything is in order now. I have sold my house; Walter, who has been with me for so many years, is retiring, and I will be joining dear friends in the south of France. My ship sails tonight.

"I am truly sorry I must go, but I know I leave Gabriel in good hands."

With her throat aching, Linda watched her mother and Paul walk slowly beside Mrs. Wentworth toward the Garden door. "I don't think I really understand any of this," she finally said to Katie in a shaking voice. "She wanted Gabriel so badly and she seemed to be so proud of him. Why should she give him to me now?"

"She can't be here to be with him any more," said Katie, "and she knows how much you care. I've known for some time she was leaving, but I didn't know she'd planned to give you Gabriel. It was a wonderful thing for her to do."

"But I don't think I can bear it," whispered Linda.

"I have the most awful feeling we'll never see her again." She turned to bury her face in Gabriel's deep silver ruff.

Katie didn't answer right away. She pretended to be busy sorting collars and leads.

She finally straightened up firmly. "Don't upset the dog," she said in a low voice. "He ought to be back on the bench." She lifted him in her arms.

"Why on earth are you carrying him?" gasped Linda as she pushed through the crowds surging through the aisles between the benches.

"Because I don't want him to get stepped on!" answered Katie breathlessly. Gabriel wiggled with pleasure and washed Katie's face enthusiastically with his broad pink tongue.

With a laughing sigh of relief, Katie put him in his crate on the bench, slipped off the lead, and snapped the door shut. Gabriel yawned, curled up, and promptly went to sleep in a tight silver ball.

Jim had followed them and he nodded to Katie, his watchful eyes on the sleeping dog. Linda hesitated a moment, wondering how she could feel so miserable after being so happy just a short time before.

"Come on," said Katie gently. "There's no use looking back. You gave Mrs. Wentworth many happy days when you let her have Gabriel last fall. Now you owe it to her, and to the dog, to look ahead." Katie smiled. "And there'll be puppies. Lots and lots of puppies. Two people have already spoken to me about breeding to Gabriel. One was the owner of that lovely bitch that was Best Opposite Sex to Gabriel this morning. Of course, the dog is yours now. These are your decisions to make."

"*Me?*" said Linda. "I don't know anything about it!"

"You can learn," Katie said comfortably. "You must study pedigrees, and bloodlines, and learn about genetics, too. I have two very good books on heredity I can lend you to start you off."

They sat down on one of the grooming tables to wait for Mrs. Fairfax and Paul to come back. "Perhaps, if you like one of the bitches particularly, you might want to take a puppy from one of Gabriel's litters instead of a stud fee. Paul and I could help you choose and you would have another young one to raise while Gabriel is being shown. . . ."

Sons and daughters of Gabriel, to carry on the Harborlight line. Linda let out her breath in a tired, happy sigh. She was beginning to feel better.

"You might want to learn how to handle the puppy yourself," Katie went on. "Lots of owners show their own dogs, you know."

137

Paul came back, and other clients came to speak to him and Katie. Linda slipped away, feeling a little guilty. It was hard to remember that Katie and Paul had several other people to worry about, and other dogs to prepare and show today, while she herself was so preoccupied with Gabriel.

She caught sight of her mother, looking smart and trim in her New York suit. "There you are!" said Mrs. Fairfax. "What would you like to do this afternoon? What have you missed in New York most of all? Would you like to go shopping?"

Linda glanced down at the dress she was wearing and tugged at the skirt. "Oh, this is all right," she said. "I'd really rather stay here at the Garden, if it's all right with you. Katie is showing Mrs. Burke's Boxer in a few minutes and I'd like to watch."

Mrs. Fairfax shook her head in pretended astonishment. "I don't believe you're the same Linda I knew when we left New York," she said with a smile.

Linda's gray eyes were serious as she turned to look across the benching area. She could just see the edge of the line of Keeshond benches where she knew Gabriel was sleeping safely, waiting for tonight.

Linda turned to smile at her mother. "I know," she said. "Now come on, let's hurry or we'll miss the class." Together, they made their way out onto the Garden floor.

Made in United States
North Haven, CT
22 April 2023

35765433R00088